Anointed Insp
Publishing
Presents

D1522116

Hope's Faith

A novel by
Raegan Dennis

Copyright © 2017 Raegan Dennis
Published by Anointed Inspirations Publishing

Note: This is a work of fiction. Names, characters, places and incidents either are products of the author's imagination or are used fictitiously. Any resemblance to actual events or locales or persons, living or dead, is entirely coincidental

Anointed Inspirations Publishing, LLC is currently accepting Urban Christian Fiction, Inspirational Romance, Inspirational Poetry, Self-Help, Memoirs, and Young Adult fiction submissions. For consideration please send manuscripts to
Anointedinspirationspublishing@gmail.com

CHAPTER 1

"You have to be kidding me." I thought out loud when I saw the two-distinct pink lines on the pregnancy test. I've got to tell Chloe I thought as I put the test down to wash my hands. Chloe and I had been best friends for the past 15 years. We met in cosmetology school and were fast friends from the time we were paired up to do manicures on each other. I stayed in the hair business and did pretty good as a full time hairstylist while she ended up going back to school and for something completely different and landed an awesome job at one of the largest imaging centers performing X Rays and different types of scans.

"Chloe please answer," I said on her voicemail after the fourth phone call.

She is probably on her way to work I thought. It was a Tuesday and I had three appointments that day. All of them were regulars so I would leave as soon as I was done. God I need you now more than ever I silently prayed to myself.

"How did I get in this mess?" I knew I was losing my mind because I kept talking to myself.

"My grace is sufficient for thee." I heard the quiet voice of God speak to me as tears streamed down my face. God must be so disappointed in me, ran through my mind s I dried my tears and began getting ready for work. Glad I had survived my day at the salon I got my purse and checked my phone to see if Chloe had called or text me.

"You leaving so soon?" Tamara one of my co-workers and best friends asked as she applied color to her client's hair.

"Yeah," I replied "I'm not feeling too good."

Tamera gave me a strange look. "You have been pretty quiet today. Are you sure that is the only thing, you not feeling well?" She was probing me for information that I wasn't ready to give.

"Look I'll be done with Mrs. Harris soon, she isn't getting a style just wearing her natural curls today. Why don't you wait around so I can do your hair, you look a hot mess today."

I looked in the mirror and had to confirm Tamera's words for myself. My caramel complexion had no makeup on to camouflage my few and I mean few flaws in my skin. I threw a pair of dark denim jeans and a fitted white t-shirt on my five foot five frame. Everyone who knew anything about me knew I rarely wore sneakers and here I was with a pair on today. Not to mention my short and sassy haircut was laying flat. And to top it all off I had on no earrings or accessories of any type. I couldn't be mad at Tamera she was only being truthful. I never came out looking this way. Even though I was attractive and many people said I didn't need makeup, I felt in my profession I had to always look the part.

Once Tamara was done with Mrs. Harris' hair and had walked her to the front she motioned for me to sit in her chair. Leslie, another stylist who worked with us came in and looked at the two of us and rolled her eyes before speaking.

"Hey how are you guys doing?"

"Good," Tamera and I said in unison.

Leslie made it clear she didn't care for Tamara or me. We had been in the industry much longer than her and had a much bigger clientele. We both worked at the salon full time and had no need for another job. However, Leslie had only been out of school for two years and hadn't really built a loyal client base. She worked part time at a clothing store to pay her bills. When I tried to take Leslie under my wing when she came to the salon almost a year ago and show her some industry tricks to help build a clientele she not so nicely let me know she didn't need the help of some old school hairstylist. Tamera made it known to the owner Casandra she didn't like her and we didn't need her young girl mentality at Studio Seven salon. Cassandra told Leslie everyone deserves a chance and just try to help her. Tamera was constantly telling Cassandra and myself, I told you so about Leslie.

Tamara placed a towel and cape around my neck but not before twenty inch wavy weave back in a ponytail. Tamara always wore weave of some kind she said it was the best way to get new clients in her chair. She specialized in weave and she did an amazing job at it. She stood five foot seven and had skin the color of milk chocolate. She always dressed immaculately and makeup was always flawless.

"So you want to tell me now or later what has you in a funk?" She asked me as she started putting relaxer on my hair.

I closed my eyes and all I saw was the positive pregnancy test.

"Tamara, I took a test this morning," I blurted out.

"Hope!" Tamara yelled.

"Will you please be quiet?" I asked her through clenched teeth.

"Oh I'm sorry I forgot the fake stylist is in here," she laughed out loud.

"So when you say test I assume you mean pregnancy," Tamara inquired.

"Yes," I answered with my head down in shame.

"Hold on Hope, to get pregnant you have to have sex and since you got saved and started going to church you haven't been. So how did this happen? I thought you told me that you told Shawn that you were celibate and he broke up with you." Tamara questioned me with a puzzled look on her face.

"Well," I replied feeling the shame and guilt all over again that I did when I took the test. I had to give Tamera an explanation.

"Well I kind of left some details out," I confessed to Tamara. "I slept with Shawn after he took me out for Valentine's Day. I felt so ashamed like God was looking directly at me. I was celibate for over a year and the one time I slip up I get pregnant." By this time tears were freely running down my face. "I really messed up, how can I face my pastor, my church, my parents."

Tamera gave me some tissues as I continued to talk.

"Then the father is a no good jerk who bailed because I refused to compromise my faith and my body. What if he doesn't help me with this baby or wants me to abort it?" The floodgates of my tears were really flowing now.

Tamera let me cry for a few more minutes then led me to the shampoo bowl. It actually felt good to get all of that off my chest and I was glad Tamara and I were friends at this moment more than ever. Tamara shampooed my hair and got me ready to go under the dryer. We didn't say much at the bowl because Leslie kept giving us crazy looks. We waited until I was dry and back in her chair to finish our conversation. As Tamara curled my hair she asked when was I going to tell Shawn.

"I have no idea really. I think I want to go to the doctor first and make sure everything is okay." I told her.

"Have you told Chloe?" She asked.

"I tried to call her this morning, no answer, I know she will call tonight though," I let Tamara know.

"Between me and Chloe we will support you in this. And if your church is bible based they will forgive you and support you. The bible says we must be helpers one to another," Tamara said as she put the finishing touches on my hair.

She never ceased to amaze me. Not that she wasn't a Christian she just didn't go to church as much as I did but she really did hide the word in her heart. And that's the type of friend I needed right now.

CHAPTER 2

My first prenatal appointment was mind blowing to say the least. I was more than grateful that I decided to take the whole day off because there is no way I would be able to keep my eyes open too much longer. All the paperwork I filled out made me feel like I was buying a car. I wondered if I had any blood left the way the nurse kept filling tubes. After my weight check, blood pressure, and urine sample I finally got to see Dr. Goldman. He had been my gynecologist for the past six years and he had the best bedside manner of any doctor I knew. He was referred to me by Chloe. That was a perk of having a best friend who worked in the medical field. Dr. Goldman was a short Jewish man with a huge personality.

"Hope!" He exclaimed excitedly when he walked in the exam room.

"How have you been? I was a little surprised to see you as a prenatal appointment," he said as he shook my hand.

Is that judgment I hear in his voice? I thought to myself. Maybe I should have found a new gynecologist, someone who doesn't know me. All these thoughts were overtaking my mind as the initial guilt of my mistake was trying to take control of me.

"Hope, are you alright?" Dr. Goldman asked me with much concern in his voice.

"Oh yes, just a little nervous," I quickly answered.

"New mommy nerves are common for first time mothers, no need to worry, I'm sure you will be a natural," he assured me.

"Let me get Stacey in here so we can see your baby," he said referring to one of his nurses.

Dr. Goldman left the room just in time for me to wipe away the few tears that managed to escape. Stacey and Dr. Goldman came into the exam room and Stacey instructed me to lie back and turn my head to the side so I could see the screen. She explained since it was so early in the pregnancy the doctor would be performing a transvaginal ultrasound. I can imagine the look of horror on my face because Stacey patted my hand and told me to relax it was absolutely painless.

"Do you see your baby?" Dr. Goldman asked. It really just looked like a jelly bean on the screen to me.

"Wow," was all I could manage to say.

He looked for a few more minutes and informed me that everything looked good and confirmed my due date of December twentieth. He printed a few pictures and gave me a prescription for prenatal vitamins.

"Go ahead and get dressed and I will walk you up front to make your next appointment when you are done," Stacey told me.

"I'll see you in four weeks Hope and congratulations," Dr. Goldman said as he walked out of the exam room.

I invited Chloe and Tamera over for dinner since it had been a while since we all spent time together. Also I needed support when I called Shawn to let him know about the baby. As I was cleaning my apartment and getting things ready for my dinner guests, my cell phone rang. I ran over to the kitchen counter where it was charging and froze when I saw the name on the screen. I should have known Pastor Wright would be calling me considering I hadn't stepped foot in my church since I found out about my pregnancy almost four weeks ago.

Pastor Wright was a great leader, she was very hands on with her members not to mention spiritually in tune with us. She was in her mid-fifties, but she knew how to keep up with everyone from the elderly to the children. It's not that I was avoiding her, I just wasn't ready to face her. I had to admit I did miss going to church. I'd been watching a few television ministries, but there was nothing like being in the presence of the Lord with other believers. I had made quite a few friends since I'd been there and I did miss them and I guess they missed me too because I had been receiving text messages and voicemail asking if I was okay. I picked up the phone and listened to the message Pastor Wright left.

"Hey Sweetie, this is your Pastor. I'm worried about you, I haven't seen you in quite a few Sundays. That's not like you at all, call me as soon as you can." She rattled off her phone number as if I didn't have it.

That was one thing I loved about my church and Pastor, she was not untouchable, she made herself available to all of her members. I was relieved once I listened to the message, I thought she would be angry and chastise me like a runaway child. But I heard the care and concern in her voice and knew I owed her an explanation, better yet the truth.

After I finished cleaning my apartment and put my lasagna in the oven I decided now would be a good time to return to Pastor Wright's phone call. I sat on my second story balcony with a glass of lemonade and went through my contacts in my cell phone until I came across her name. As I hit the call button I thought my heart would beat out of my chest, I was that nervous.

"Pastor Wright speaking," was all I heard and the tears just began to flow freely.

"Hope, sweetie what is wrong?" She asked me in the most calming voice." Calm down honey, I can't help you if you don't let me know what type of help you need."

I wiped my tears and prepared to let my spiritual leader know what a disappointment I was to her and God. "Pastor, I really messed up," I began as I wiped more tears from my eyes.

"We all mess up Hope, no one is perfect," She simply replied.

I took a deep breath hoping I could get out the whole story this time.

"I'm pregnant," I waited for the backlash that never came, actually I got a chuckle.

"Is that all, Hope?" She chuckled, more like laughed this time.

"Pastor!" I exclaimed totally caught off guard. "How can you laugh?" I asked.

"I can laugh because God is good God is forgiving, and God doesn't make mistakes," She said with complete confidence. "The young man that came to church with you a few times, is he the father?" My pastor questioned me.

"Unfortunately, he is. The crazy part is I only slept with him one time and look at the mess I'm in. I really liked him, I thought he could have been the one," I told my pastor as bitter memories started to resurface about our breakup.

A few seconds of silence went by before Pastor Wright spoke. "Do you know how the bible speaks of being unequally yoked? Young people living for Christ must be careful not to get involved with people who are not seeking the kingdom of God for themselves. Just because they throw a few lines your way, oh I love the Lord, I go to church, does not make them saved. They even go to a few services with you, now you are really impressed and it's easy to sweet talk you. Oh don't let him be fine honey."

We both began to laugh at that.

"That is a trap set up by the enemy to get your focus off God," she said with true authority. "Now are you still seeing this young man?" She asked me.

"No," I answered. "After the deed was done, I felt so guilty I told him that could never happen again, it was not worth my relationship with God. He told me he didn't understand if I did it that one time, I should be able to continue, it wasn't a big deal if God was so forgiving. I have not heard from him since then."

Pastor Wright sighed. "The big deal is your salvation, you did the right thing sweetie. And that guilt you felt was you being convicted by the holy spirit. I'm so glad you were led by the holy spirit and put an end to it. I'm proud of you, this is not the end of the world, you learned a tough lesson, this means you are growing in Christ. The Lord will see you through this pregnancy, just trust His plan for your life." The word my pastor just spoke gave me a lot to think about. "Hope have you told the father he's going to be a father?" She questioned me.

"I intend to tonight, I'm a little nervous," I told her.

"Well you have every right to be considering how he treated you, but remember this is in God's hands," Pastor Wright reassured me. "Just be careful with him, I don't trust him. It's something about him," She confessed.

"Why didn't you tell me before?" I asked.

"You know what?" She began. "When he stopped coming after only four or five services, I knew he wouldn't be around for long. But I want you to remember that God forgives our sins, that's why Jesus Christ died on the cross for us. And one last thing Hope, don't stay out of church like that again, we are here to help you, not judge you. Love you, see you Sunday," Pastor Wright said.

"I love you too, thank you so much Pastor, and I promise I'll be there Sunday." I said before I hung up, my other line was ringing with a private number and anyone who knew anything about me knew I didn't answer private numbers.

I didn't realize how long I was on the phone until I walked in my apartment from the balcony and smelled the unmistakable aroma of burnt lasagna.

"No, no, no!" I yelled. I ran into the kitchen and pulled my blackened lasagna out of the oven.

Smoke quickly filled the kitchen and the smoke detector went off. I put the pan on top of the stove and went to open the windows. I grabbed a chair from the dining room table, pulled it into the hall and stood on it to take the smoke detector down so I could stop that dreadful sound. As I was getting down off the chair, I lost my footing and fell off the chair on the floor. I immediately started to cry. When I fell, I hit my back on the door frame pretty hard and I was in a lot of pain.

I was trying hard not to panic as I tried my best to get up so I could get to my phone. I tried to pull myself up using the wall for leverage, but that proved to be very painful. All I could think about was my unborn baby.

"Lord, please don't let anything happen to my baby." I cried out loud.

I finally managed to pull myself up, but the pain was unbearable. It seemed like it took forever to make it to the dining room table where my phone was, I picked it up and dialed Chloe.

She and Tamara should be here any minute but I needed them this minute.

"Hope we are right around the corner, you know it's Tamara's fault we are late," Chloe joked as she answered the phone.

"I fell and I'm hurting pretty badly and I need you guys to get here now," I told her trying not to sound as worried as I was.

"Oh my God! Are you okay? What happened?" Chloe was asking me question after question with no time to answer anything. I then heard her relaying what I'd just told her to Tamara.

"We are about three minutes away, when we get there we will take you to the hospital," Chloe informed me.

"I'm hurting really bad and I'm worried about the baby," I began to cry again.

"Try to stay calm Hope, we are almost there." Chloe said.

I slowly made my way to my beige sofa and laid down with the phone to my ear.

"Okay we are on the way up," Chloe said before we hung up the phone.

I heard the lock on the front door being turned. We all had spare keys to each other's homes in case of an emergency.

"What is that smell?" Tamara practically yelled walking in the door.

"I kind of burned the lasagna." I told my them. "That's actually how I fell," I continued as I slowly sat up.

"Well you can tell us about it in the car," Chloe said as she began to close and lock the windows I'd opened.

Tamara went to my bedroom to retrieve my purse and then came back out to help me up. My two best friends helped me down the one flight of stairs that led to the parking lot and helped me into Tamara's car, we were soon on our way to the hospital. Thank God for friends like this.

When we arrived at the emergency room I was more than grateful to see it was not busy and even more grateful that I was able to go right back. The nurse told Tamara and Chloe that she would call them back as soon as I got into a room, she was only checking my vitals.

I was instructed to take a seat in the hard, cold seat in the corner. The nurse put an arm pressure cuff on my left arm and put a thermometer in my mouth. My temperature was normal but my blood pressure was extremely high.

"So what brings you in this evening?" The nurse asked as she put my vital signs in the computer.

I told her how I fell off the chair turning my smoke alarm off and that I was ten weeks pregnant. I also let her know I hurt my back because I hit the door frame and I was in excruciating pain.

She asked me to lift my shirt so she could take a look at my back. She touched where I assumed a bruise would be.

"Is that painful?" The nurse asked.

"Very," I replied as I pulled my shirt back down.

"Have you started prenatal care yet? I know it is still early in the pregnancy," she asked me while putting more information in the computer.

"I actually had my first prenatal appointment this morning," I informed the nurse.

"Okay, that may eliminate some of the bloodwork. Who is your Ob?" She asked.

"Dr. Goldman at Memorial OB/GYN." I answered.

"Who is your primary care physician?" She asked.

"Dr. Davis at First Family Practice." I answered feeling as though the questions would not stop.

I finally looked at the nurse's name tag and learned her name was Mary. She was an older lady with a graying hairline. Her hair was in a tight bun. She had the most beautiful olive colored skin I'd ever seen. She wore no makeup and the only jewelry she wore was a simple gold wedding band on her left hand. Nurse Mary asked me a few more questions about my medical history before she led me to a room.

"Get completely undressed, under garments included and put the gown on that's on the bed. It fastens in the back. I'll give you about ten minutes before I send your friends in and I hope you feel better dear," she said before she walked out of the room.

As Nurse Mary was walking out another nurse came in and introduced herself as Cynthia. She let me know she would be taking care of me while I was in the emergency room. I was glad to have my friends at the hospital with me because I really needed the support. Tamara was sitting in the chair right beside my bed texting on her phone and Chloe was sitting next to her flipping channels on TV.

Cynthia came in and let me know they were sending me to ultrasound, would be giving me something for pain, and would be monitoring my blood pressure.

"We are a little concerned about how high your blood pressure is Hope. Have you had any past issues with high blood pressure or does it run in your family?" She asked me while looking at my right arm for a good vein to start an IV.

"My mom has had some issues with high blood pressure, but mine has never been high," I told her.

"Often times when you are in extreme pain it will cause your blood pressure to elevate, but this is something we want your doctor to monitor throughout your pregnancy," Cynthia informed me. She finished hooking up my IV. and started fluids. "How would you rate your pain, ten being the worst?" She asked me.

"About a nine, I fell pretty hard," I responded.

She then had me turn on my side so she could examine the bruise I'm sure was forming at this point. When I lay back on my back I realized laying on my side was more comfortable so I turned back on my side.

Cynthia then began asking more questions. "Other than your back where are you experiencing pain?"

As soon as she asked Tamara and Chloe both stopped what they were doing and looked at me. I knew they were as worried as I was at that point.

"Well the bottom of my stomach hurts really bad," I answered Cynthia.

I then noticed my two best friends exchanged worried looks which only put me in panic mode. Cynthia continued with her questions that were only making me nervous.

"Are you experiencing any bleeding or spotting at all?" She asked and I noticed her voice began to take on a more compassionate tone.

I looked at my two friends and then the nurse before I answered. "I did notice a little blood when I was changing clothes. What does that mean? Will I lose my baby?"

I was definitely in full panic mode. I just got used to the idea of having a baby and being a mom and it seemed as if my baby may not survive this short ten weeks. Tamera grabbed my left hand in an attempt to comfort me.

"Calm down Hope, we don't know anything yet," she said trying her best not to match my hysterical tone.

Chloe got out of her chair to move closer to me and Tamera and looked directly at Nurse Cynthia.

"How long will it be before Hope goes to ultrasound?" Chloe asked the nurse.

"Well, I wanted to give her something for pain to see if that brings her blood pressure down first," she responded with much concern in her voice.

We always joked that Chloe was the mother hen of our group but times like this that came in handy.

"What will you be giving her for pain?" She asked with her hand on her hip.

Nurse Cynthia did not seem to mind the line of questioning that Chloe was throwing her way.

"Morphine through an I.V., it should work quickly and it is safe for the baby," She said the last part about morphine being safe as if she knew one of us would question the safety. Tamara looked at Chloe with doubt in her eyes but Chloe just nodded her head as if to say the nurse was right. With Chloe being in the medical field I knew she had enough knowledge not to let anything happen to me or my baby.

The morphine was definitely doing its job because the pain was subsiding and I was beginning to drift off in a peaceful sleep. I don't know how long I was asleep when Cynthia came back in the room to take my blood pressure again and let us know someone would be taking me to ultrasound momentarily.

"One of you ladies can go to ultrasound with Hope," she looked at my friends as she spoke.

Of course Chloe spoke up first. "I'll go with you so I can make sure the ultrasound technique is on point," she said that with laughter in her voice but Tamera and I both knew that she was serious.

The blood pressure machine beeped and we all turned to look at the monitor.

"It's still a little higher than we want it." Nurse Cynthia said as she room the cuff off of my left arm. "As soon as we see the ultrasound I will be calling your doctor, blood pressure is serious on its own, even more so in pregnancy," she said.

All of this was really scaring me, I didn't know what to expect or how to handle everything that was happening. My thoughts were interrupted by a knock on the door. A young man wearing teal blue scrubs came in.

"I'm here to take you to ultrasound." The young man informed me.

Chloe got up to follow us and I was silently thanking God that she was there for me. There was no way I could have done this on my own and I was so grateful my two best friends were there with me through this whole ordeal.

As the young man maneuvered my bed down the hospital hallway and Chloe was holding my hand I was praying silently for my unborn baby. We arrived at a room that said ultrasound on the door and a short woman who looked to be in her mid-twenties was at the door waiting on us.

"Hope Daniels?" The ultrasound tech questioned.

"That's me." I replied.

"Can you verify your birthday for me?" She asked me. "Eight, nine, eighty," I quickly answered ready to see what was going on with my baby.

Once the bed was in position for the ultrasound technique to do her job she let me know she would be doing two ultrasounds, one on the abdomen and one transvaginal. I was not looking forward to this considering I just went through this earlier today, but I would endure anything for my child.

It was eerily quiet as the tech performed my ultrasound. I could tell that Chloe was trying her best to study what was going on the screen as she continued to hold my hand for support. The tech was saving images and typing in a brief descriptions on each one. I didn't know what any of it meant and to be honest I was afraid to ask. Every time I looked at Chloe she had an intense look on her face and that made me even more afraid.

The tech finally broke the silence. "Is this your first baby?" She asked.

"Yes this is my first," I answered.

"Okay Hope, I'm going to perform the transvaginal portion of the ultrasound now," she said.

I already knew what to expect since I had this exact procedure done earlier, but that did not help my nervous state of mind. I must say that it was very uncomfortable and Chloe must have noticed the look on my face because she just began to rub the back of my hand.

"We are all done," the tech announced.

I immediately tried to sit up but Chloe stopped me.

"Just lay back and rest sweetie," she said.

Now I was really worried Chloe was using terms of endearment which usually meant something was wrong.

"What is going on?" I asked with tears in my eyes.

The ultrasound tech jumped in with what I'm sure was a script for moments like this. "I'm going to send these images to the OB on call and he can explain everything to you."

At that point she wheeled me back to my room as Chloe followed. Tamera put her phone down and came to stand beside the bed as soon as it was back in place.

"How did it go?" She asked sounding just as worried as I did.

"We don't know anything for sure just yet." Chloe answered.

I turned to look at Chloe. She performed MRI's, CT scans, and X-rays for an imaging center and had been for the last six years. I knew she could tell something because she started off as an ultrasound tech at a small private practice about eight years ago.

"Please tell me something Chloe." I practically begged.

"Sweetie, I haven't done an ultrasound in years. All I see lately is broken bones and bad joints," she said with a slight chuckle trying to lighten the mood.

I could tell she knew something but I wasn't going to get it out of her.

"Look, just try to rest, that is what is important now, stressing is not good for you or the baby," Chloe said in a tone that let me know the subject was no longer up for discussion.

CHAPTER 3

At this point everything was a blur because Nurse Cynthia came back in to give me another dose of morphine. I'm not sure how much time had passed when I heard Tamara and Chloe introduce themselves to someone. I opened my eyes and sat up in the bed to see who they were talking to.

"I'm Dr. Phillips. How are you feeling Hope?" The young blonde doctor asked as she walked toward the bed.

"Not so good." I answered the sleep still evident in my voice.

"Well I have called Dr. Goldman and informed him you were here. We are really concerned with your blood pressure. Also I took a look at your ultrasound." Dr. Phillips was starting to make me nervous as she spoke. "It looks like you are threatening a miscarriage. At this point, there is a fifty-fifty chance that the baby will survive. You are very early in the pregnancy and it seems you took quite a fall. The next forty-eight hours are crucial and I need you on complete bed rest. Dr. Goldman wants me to admit you and get you up to a room so we can observe you and he will be here to see you tomorrow."

It seemed as though Dr. Phillips gave me more information than I could digest. There was nothing that I could do to stop the tears from freely flowing down my cheeks. Everything happened so fast. One minute I was asleep in a room in the emergency department, the next minute I was put in a wheelchair and taken to a room and admitted to the hospital. Since I was no longer in the emergency department of the hospital, Cynthia was no longer my nurse.

The third nurse I had seen since arriving at the hospital walked in and introduced herself. "Good evening ladies, I'm Bianca, I'll be taking care of you tonight."

Bianca had skin the color of milk chocolate. Her hair was cut in long layers a little past her shoulders with a few golden highlights streaked through. She had slender build and appeared to be a little taller than the average female. As I was looking at Nurse Bianca, I couldn't help but to wonder why she didn't pursue a modeling career.

"Your hair is gorgeous." I told my new nurse.

"Thank you, but that should be the least of our worries." She said with a humble smile.

Of course mama bear Chloe piped in. "My two best friends here are two of the best hairstylist in Charlotte so they are always critiquing everyone's hair, even when it may not be the most appropriate timing."

Of course Tamera still had to voice her opinion. "Your hair is fabulous, Hope just made an honest observation."

Chloe gave her a look that could kill that made us both be quiet.

"I appreciate the compliments ladies, I really do, but let's get Hope settled so she can concentrate on resting, that is the most important thing we need to focus on." Bianca stated with a firmness in her voice that let us know she meant business. "Now only one of your friends can stay the night, hospital policy, so we need to make a decision," she informed us while looking at all three of us.

Chloe was the first to talk "It makes sense for me to stay since I have a lot of PTO I need to use and Tamera you have clients tomorrow and you may need to call Hope's clients and get in who you can and move the others around." That was just like Chloe to become the boss whenever there was a crisis.

At this point I appreciated her thought process because I hadn't thought about work or my clients. All I could think about was keeping my baby safe. Even though this was a true emergency, a woman and her hair is not something to take lightly. Tamara agreed with Chloe's action plan and it made perfect sense to me as well. I informed Tamara that my appointments were all on the computerized appointment book along with any color formulas she may need for my clients. She came over to my bed and gave me a quick hug and kissed my cheek.

"I'm out of here guys, make sure you call me if anything changes and I love you sisters." she said as she walked out of my hospital room.

Just as I was drifting back off to sleep, I felt the blood pressure cuff tightening. I looked up to see Bianca checking my vital signs.

"I am so sorry to wake you sweetie, I just need to get your vitals and Dr. Phillips wants to see if your blood pressure has dropped at all." She told me as she placed a thermometer under my tongue. "Blood pressure is still a little high one-sixty over eighty-five." Bianca stated while taking the thermometer out of my mouth. "No fever, ninety-seven point five, perfect." She said.

She then asked me to rate my pain, ten being the worst and zero being no pain at all.

I thought about how my stomach was cramping and how my back was aching. "I would say about a seven." I answered.

Bianca looked at me with her hand on her cheek as if she was deep in thought. "Well, at this point I just need you to rest, that is the best way to protect the baby." She told me with much concern evident in her voice.

As Bianca was leaving, Chloe got up from the couch she had been sleeping on. "How are you feeling sweetie?" She asked while holding my hand.

Of course I began to cry, I was so overwhelmed.

"You know what I just realized Hope?" Chloe asked as if I already knew the answer. "The whole time we have been at the hospital we have not petitioned God, we have yet to pray."

Once again, I realized how awesome my friendship was with Chloe and Tamera. I was so upset I forgot to do what counted most and that was talk to my heavenly father, thank God Chloe was here.

"Merciful Father I come to you on behalf of my dear sister Hope. She needs a touch from you as never before. Lord help Hope forgive herself and allow her to understand that children are a heritage from You a reward from You according to Psalms 127. Reduce her stress level oh God that her blood pressure may regulate. Oh God dissipate all pain from her body. Give her a peace that surpasses all understanding. Give her strength to carry this baby full term and allow him or her to be healthy and whole. Let your will be done in Hope's life and in the new life of this baby. In the mighty name of Jesus Amen!"

CHAPTER 4

I was really confused because everyone kept telling me to rest, but is virtually impossible to get any real rest in the hospital. First, let's talk about how uncomfortable the beds are, no matter how much adjusting you do. Not to mention when you do get semi comfortable, the nurse is coming in to check your temperature and blood pressure. Since I knew that I would not be sleeping anytime soon, I picked up my phone from the bedside table to see if I had any missed calls or texts. I must have been moving around too much because Chloe sat up and began rubbing her eyes.

"I didn't mean to wake you," I apologetically said.

"Who sleeps in hospitals anyway," was Chloe's response.

"That is funny because I was thinking the same thing," I told her.

Chloe got up from her makeshift bed on the couch that rested on the wall right under the only window in the room. We were on the eighth floor of the hospital so you could see the skyline of uptown Charlotte clearly. The lights of the buildings were beautiful and under different circumstances I would have enjoyed the view.

"And why are you up anyway?" Chloe asked breaking our brief moment of silence.

I just looked at Chloe for a moment before I answered.

Chloe was very low maintenance compared to Tamara and myself. She normally wore her hair in a messy bun or ponytail, but she decided to do something different and got her hair done in micro braids. They actually looked great on her. She only stood five three, making her the shortest of our trio, with skin the color of honey.

"Hello Hope, are you spacing out on me?" Chloe questioned .

"Oh, I'm sorry, since I was up, I was just going to check my phone," I told Chloe.

But as soon as I got that sentence out, I began to have painful cramping. The look on my face or the sound of my voice, or maybe both must have alarmed Chloe because she was beside my bed in an instant. She grabbed my hand and asked if I was okay.

"I'm starting to cramp again, I'm really scared, what if my baby doesn't make it? Am I being punished for how my baby was conceived?"

Again I found myself in tears, I have never cried this much, but I have never felt such fear.

Chloe grabbed some tissue from the tissue box on the bedside table and began to wipe my face.

"Hope, you have to calm down, take a deep breath," Chloe instructed, trying her best to calm me down. "The Lord will not leave you, nor will He forsake you, many are the tribulations of the righteous, but the Lord delivered them from them all. You have to believe that for yourself and our baby. This is not the time to fall apart, this is the time to stand on the word of God. A lot of women have been in this same situation yet carried healthy babies to term, but that can't happen if you are stressed." Chloe said this with so much authority, I should have known not to question her, but I did.

"What about the women that do miscarry? How do they go on after losing a baby? It's not like I can just try again, I'm not married, I don't even have a boyfriend. What if this my only chance to be a mother? I would not able to live with myself knowing ultimately it was my fault if I miscarry.

I can't believe I stood on that chair, what was I thinking?" I was really on a roll and ready to be the guest of honor at my own pity party.

I believe Chloe was getting a little frustrated with me. Instead of getting the comforting response that I was hoping for, I got the sound of the bathroom door closing. It is no secret that I do not do well with crisis situations, I tend to think of the worst possible scenario and play it over and over in my mind. The longer I sat there alone, the more I thought, the more I thought about what Chloe just said. I knew she was trying extremely hard to be sensitive to my situation. Any other time she would have been more than happy to tell me, or anyone else exactly how things should be and why they should be that way. If I truly trusted God why was it so hard for me to believe what the word of God said? Did I not have faith? This is something I have struggled with since I gave my life to Christ.

I will say I have faith, I will talk to others about how their faith in God can sustain them through any situation. Why is it so hard for me to apply that to myself?

Chloe came out of the bathroom drying tears of her own. I was in complete shock because she rarely showed true emotion and she very rarely cried. I must have really struck a nerve. Chloe moved one of the chairs closer to the bed and pushed the button to call the nurse.

"How can we help you?" One of the nurses responded on the intercom.

Chloe responded before I could even open my mouth. "Is there any way we can get anything for pain? Hope is experiencing some cramping."

Just as I was about to protest Bianca walked into the room.

"That was quick," I said as Bianca came over to check my vitals.

"It is actually pretty empty in here tonight, I was standing at the nurse's station when you called. Once I do this set of vitals, I'll get you some more pain meds in your IV. If you are hungry I can get you a snack, but I really want you to rest," Bianca said as she put the arm pressure cuff on me. We all looked as the numbers changed to see where they would settle.

"Okay we are making a little progress, your blood pressure did drop a little." After Bianca said that I think we all breathed a sigh of relief. "I will be right back with your pain meds, unless you are hungry, I can grab you a snack first," she said on her way to the door.

I was actually hungry, but I think with all that happened I forgot about eating. "A snack would be great," I said to Bianca. She asked me if a peanut butter and jelly sandwich would be fine and I gladly told her yes.

"I'll be right back" she said as she walked out of the room.

"Chloe, are you okay? I didn't mean to upset you, you know how I go into panic mode and start freaking out." I asked her looking directly in her eyes.

She looked down and let out a sigh before she began to speak. "Hope, there is something I need to tell you, and I'm not sure how. No one knows, not Tamera, not my family, just one other person." I was not sure what to expect or how to react. I hadn't seen her this emotional since her grandmother passed away ten years ago.

Before she could go on, Bianca walked back into the room with my peanut butter and jelly sandwich and my pain medicine. Even though I was in pain, I really wanted to hear what Chloe had to say, but I knew I would have to wait because once the medicine took effect I would be sleep in no time. I took the sandwich from my nurse and took a few bites and realized I wasn't hungry after all and put the rest on the table beside the bed. That is when it hit me that I never checked my phone. I picked it up while Bianca flushed my IV and gave me the pain medicine.

I immediately felt warm all over as the pain began to dissipate. I unlocked my screen and saw that I had several missed calls and texts. Of course I was thinking it was mainly clients wanting to make appointments. I was surprised to see that I had four missed calls from private numbers. My mom had also called, I wasn't so surprised about that, I have been avoiding her for the past few weeks. I knew once I talked to her she would want me to come see her and my dad and I was not ready to face them. Before I could even check my voicemail or text messages, I felt myself battling sleep, without even putting up a fight I put my phone down closed my eyes and allowed sleep to win.

CHAPTER 5

The next morning I woke up to an older woman bringing me breakfast. "Good morning, I'm Claire from food services, I have breakfast for you." I sat up and asked her what time it was.

"Oh it's seven o'clock dear, we eat pretty early around here," she said with a gentle smile.

She lifted the cover off the plate to reveal French toast, turkey bacon and scrambled eggs. There was also two small cartons of orange juice and a cup of coffee with cream and sugar on the side. I was pretty impressed with my breakfast, but the real test would be how it tasted. And considering I did not eat much yesterday I was starving.

"Enjoy your breakfast dear and if you are going to be around for lunch call and put your order in from the menu I left on your tray, but it takes about an hour so don't wait until you get too hungry. You are eating for two," Claire said with the most genuine smile.

"Thank you Ms. Claire," I said as I prepared my coffee the way I liked it.

"You are welcome," she said as she walked toward the door. All of a sudden she stopped and turned back around heading for my bed. "I don't normally do this at work, but I have to be obedient to what the Lord has put in my spirit."

My heart began to race the same way it did the very first time Pastor Wright prophesied over my life, so I knew that what she was about to say would be coming straight from the God we both served.

Ms. Claire grabbed my hand and closed her eyes. She immediately began speaking in her heavenly language. I knew the holy spirit was present in that hospital room. I didn't realize I was crying until I felt the tears go past my chin.

She opened her eyes and looked at me and smiled. "God has forgiven you, when will you forgive yourself? Children are a heritage from the Lord and it is a privilege when God chooses you to become a mother. Let God be God in your life, replace your fear with faith and you will come out victorious."

I was truly amazed at this moment, this woman doesn't know me or anything about me, but God does and he sent a word just for me. "Thank you," I said through my tears, but this time they were not tears of sorrow, but tears of joy.

"If you are still here when my shift ends, I will come by and check on you." She said as she began to walk toward the door. She turned around and said one last thing before she left. "Remember that forgiveness and faith are your weapons."

I wiped my tears and prepared to dig into my breakfast. Just as I was about to put the first bite of French toast in my mouth Chloe woke up.

"How are you feeling?" She asked.

I put my fork down and smiled at her.

"You are smiling, that is definitely an improvement from last night," Chloe said as she got off of the couch.

"I just had the most amazing experience, God literally just sent a word just for me to this hospital room," I told my friend.

"I thought I heard talking but I thought I was dreaming, tell me about it as soon as I use the bathroom, I can't hold it another second." I could barely hear what she said because she was already in the bathroom.

Glad that I was finally able to start my breakfast, I savored that first bite of French toast. For hospital food, it wasn't bad at all, or it could have been how hungry I was that made this food taste so good. The goal was to eat as much as I could while Chloe was in the bathroom, I knew once she came out and I started to tell her about my experience with Ms. Claire, I would not be thinking about food. I had not been this excited about God in a while and I knew that was my fault. I have been allowing guilt and shame to set in instead of allowing God to carry my burdens.

Just as I was finishing my breakfast, Bianca came in with another nurse who she introduced me to as Allison.

"Hi Hope, I'm going to be taking over for Bianca, I just need a set of vitals and Dr. Goldman should be here in about an hour. He gets to decide if you get to go home or stay with us," Allison said as she walked toward my bed.

Allison was talking to Bianca when Chloe came out of the bathroom.

"Oh my goodness!" Chloe exclaimed. "Allison, I haven't seen you in years," she said with excitement evident in her voice.

"Chloe, wow, it is so good to see you." Allison's enthusiasm matched Chloe's.

"Allison and I used to work together at Ballantyne OB/GYN back when I was doing ultrasounds, she was one of the nurses," Chloe explained.

"This is your Hope? It is really a small world. I've heard so much about you, all good I can assure," Allison said as she prepared to get my vital signs.

"Chloe where are you working now?" Allison asked looking at the thermometer.

"I'm over at Midtown Imaging center, I mainly perform MRI's and a few CT scans, I really enjoy it, it's definitely not as hectic as working in obstetrics and gynecology," Chloe answered.

They both shared a laugh and I was happy to see my friend laugh, I felt like at times she took life too seriously.

"What do you rate your pain level, one being no pain and ten being the worst pain you've experienced in your life?" Allison asked me.

"About a six," I said as I studied the faces of the two nurses and my best friend.

Everyone looked a little intense to me and when I realized why, I tried my best not to match their worried looks. When I looked at the blood pressure reading, I was shocked to see that my blood pressure was back up again from last night. I recalled the words Ms. Claire spoke about faith earlier and decided this was not the time to worry.

Allison was the first to speak, "I can't say for sure, but I'm pretty positive that Dr. Goldman may want to keep you another day or so. Have you ever had blood pressure issues in the past?"

That was what was so strange to me, I never had high blood pressure, it has been a battle for my mom for years, but not me. "No I haven't, my blood pressure has always been normal, my mom has been on blood pressure medicine for years," I let Allison know.

"We will let you get some rest while we wait on Dr. Goldman. I'll be in soon but if you need me before then, just call the nurse's station," she said as she and Bianca prepared to leave.

Bianca was the next to speak. "If you are still here, I will see you tonight."

They walked out of the room leaving me and Chloe alone.

"Now that we have a few minutes to ourselves, tell me about what had you smiling this morning." Chloe said as she sat on the foot of the bed.

"I will, as soon as I use the bathroom," I said as I swung my feet off of the side of the bed.

I pulled the pole that my IV fluids were hooked to into the bathroom with me, not because I wanted to, but when you are hooked up to an IV you have no choice. When I used the bathroom, I noticed that I was still spotting and knew that I would have to inform my nurse. I have never been pregnant before but I knew that bleeding could mean there was a potential problem. I made up in my mind that I would do whatever I had to do to carry my baby for as long as possible.

As I was washing my hands I looked at myself in the mirror. Times like this I was so grateful I kept a pixie cut because it still looked pretty good, even with me not tying it up last night. I slowly made my way back into my room and noticed someone left me a clean gown along with a toothbrush, toothpaste and a few other necessary toiletries so that I could take a much needed shower.

"No ma'am," Chloe practically yelled. "You think you slick, I know you Hope, you are going to tell me what happened before you get in the shower," she said.

And yes, she did know me and that was exactly what I was going to say, but I was busted so I just sat on the bed, adjusted the back so I could sit up. I got as comfortable as I could and began telling Chloe what happened when Ms. Claire brought my breakfast. I was still excited about that experience and how God used a total stranger to speak into my life. Once I was done sharing every detail about my morning encounter, Chloe got up from the foot of the bed and gave me a hug.

"Girl you going to have me shouting all over this hospital," she said releasing our hug.

"Ms. Claire said she would stop by when she got off if I was still here, so you can meet her then. She has that grandmother loving spirit about her that makes you want to be in her presence." I smiled thinking of the older woman. "But in the meantime, I'm going to take my shower before my doctor gets here." I gathered everything that was left for me and started the short walk to the shower. I turned around when Chloe started laughing.

"What is funny?" I asked.

"The nurse has to unhook you from your IV" she chuckled.

I didn't say a word, I just gave her a look that let her know I didn't find a thing funny.

Chloe had already paged the nurse's station and told them I needed assistance.

"I need to talk to the nurse anyway," I said as I thought about the spotting I saw when I used the bathroom earlier.

Now it was Chloe's turn to give me a look. Before she could even ask what was wrong I told her about the spotting.

"You definitely need to mention that to Allison and your doctor. The more information they have, the better they can help you," was Chloe's response.

It always amazed me how something as simple as taking a shower can make you feel so much better. I came out of the bathroom refreshed and ready to tackle whatever Dr. Goldman told me. That little bit of time alone did me a world of good. I was able to talk to God in a way I felt like I didn't have the right to since I found out I was pregnant.

I literally felt a burden lift once I started praying for myself and my unborn child. I could not believe I almost allowed guilt and shame keep me from connecting with God. That is how the enemy works, and I almost fell for it.

I noticed my bed was made and the table beside it had been cleaned. Since I can be a little obsessive compulsive about cleanliness that made my mood even better. I was tired of being in bed so I opted to sit in the recliner.

That's when I noticed Chloe wasn't in my room. I assumed she ran home to shower and change or to find some food. I was enjoying my alone time but I decided to call her and make sure everything was alright. When I picked up my phone I was shocked by all the missed calls and text messages. I opted to check those after I talked to Chloe, it would give me something to do.

"Where are you?" I said into the phone after Chloe picked up on the second ring.

"Well excuse me for wanting to not look like yesterday. I ran home to take a shower change and get YOU and I some things we may need just in case they keep you another night," she said apparently proud of herself.

That is why Chloe was the mama bear, she always thought with the end in mind when Tamara and myself lived in the moment. We definitely needed her to balance us out.

"Thank you, you know I was not thinking that far ahead," I told her.

"You know I got you sister, plus I know how long your showers take so I figured I'd have plenty of time," Chloe said.

I knew it was a jab at me, my friends always complained about me being the last one ready. They even started telling me to be places thirty minutes early just to make sure I was on time.

We ended our phone call with Chloe promising to be back within the hour. I was hoping she would be back by the time my doctor came. I knew she would ask the right questions and I honestly just wanted her to be by my side.

CHAPTER 6

Allison informed me that Dr. Goldman was running behind because he had an emergency C-section and another patient in labor. That was fine with me because it gave me time to check my voicemail and respond to my text messages. I looked at the text messages first which were mostly from my clients with well wishes. My clients didn't know that I was pregnant yet and I wanted to keep it that way when I first found out. But I'm so glad I didn't feel like that anymore. Once I made it out of this hospital I would let them all know, that would only be fair so they could make arrangements to keep their hair done while I was out on maternity leave. As I was scrolling I saw a message from an unsaved number that piqued my interest. When I opened the message and read it I didn't know what to think.

This is Shawn. Call me it's really important. I need to speak to you ASAP!

What could Shawn possibly want to talk to me about? The wheels in my mind were turning. I knew I had to talk to him and the plan was to tell him last night, but apparently with the current situation that didn't happen. Mentally I wasn't prepared to deal with Shawn right now. My focus was on doing whatever I had to do to carry my baby to term.

Moving on to my missed calls I noticed more missed calls from a private number. Now it was starting to make sense, maybe Shawn had been trying to contact me. I still didn't understand why, when we ended things it was pretty final.

When I checked my voicemail I wasn't surprised to see that my mom had left me another message. Cassandra, the owner of the salon left a message to say Tamara had filled her in and she was praying for me and to call her if I needed anything. The next message floored me and I'm sure it would not help my blood pressure. Just as I was about to replay it to make sure I heard correctly Chloe walked into the room carrying two overnight bags.

"I'm back sis," she said while putting the bags in the closet beside the couch.

"Chloe, you need to listen to this voicemail." I was barely able to get the words out.

She just took the phone out of my hand and pressed play then put it on speaker.

"Miss Hope, I'm not sure what you think you have with my husband Shawn, but I'm going to need you to leave him alone. He is my husband, he isn't going anywhere and if I find out you still dealing with my husband it won't be good for you boo, consider this your first and last warning."

Chloe and I just looked at each other before I began to cry. Chloe let me cry for a few minutes before she said anything. I'm sure she was in as much shock as I was.

"This is not the time to get hysterical, your blood pressure is already elevated, you being this upset will only make it worse," Chloe said while rubbing my back.

I absolutely could not believe that I was pregnant by a married man. I knew things could be complicated with me and Shawn, but this is not what I was expecting. I was so confused, where was this wife while we were dating? And if he had a wife why was he stressing me about sex. He could have been getting that from her.

Now I'm here pregnant and I definitely don't know now if he will want to be a part of this child's life. Lord, what have I gotten myself into?

The more I thought the harder I cried. I don't believe in abortion, but maybe that would be the best solution. As fast as that thought entered my mind it left. I wanted my baby regardless of the circumstances.

"Whatever happens, you know God is in control. Let's get you cleaned up before someone comes in, I'm pretty sure it's time for your vitals to be checked." Chloe was trying her best to calm me down.

I went to the bathroom to wash my face. When I looked in the mirror I didn't know who was staring back at me. My eyes were red and puffy, my pixie cut was laying flat, I just was not myself. On top of that I felt a headache trying to surface. I had to pull it together, if not for myself, then for my baby. As I was about to leave the bathroom I felt something warm running down my leg. I pulled up my nightgown and saw it was blood. I went from spotting to bleeding in a matter of minutes.

"Chloe, call the nurse." I yelled as I adjusted my nightgown. I was washing my hands when Chloe came into the bathroom.

"I paged for a nurse, Allison will be here soon, what's wrong?" She asked with a worried look on her face.

"I'm bleeding, not spotting," I said. I was so scared I didn't want to move for fear that the slightest movement would cause more bleeding.

"Let's get you in bed," Chloe held onto my arm and helped me walk the short distance from the bathroom to the bed. Just as I was getting situated in bed Allison walked in.

"Let's get a set of vitals on you, it was almost that time anyway," Allison said as she prepared to take my temperature and blood pressure.

Before I could even open my mouth, Chloe was filling Allison in on why she paged her. "Hope went from spotting to bleeding. Do you have any idea how long it will be before Dr. Goldman comes to check on her?"

The blond haired blue eyed nurse looked at me sympathetically before she spoke. "Well he's done with the C-section and just went to check on his patient in labor, so it should be really soon."

My temperature was normal, but the numbers that were displayed on the blood pressure machine were a reason to worry. My blood pressure was the highest it had been since arriving last night. I'm pretty sure hearing the voice of Shawn's wife put me over the edge. I remembered what Chloe said about telling the doctors and nurses as much information as I could to receive the best medical care.

"I'm starting to get a really intense headache," I said as I closed my eyes because the lights were starting to make my headache worse. Someone turned the light off and I was grateful for that. Allison and Chloe were having a conversation as if I wasn't in the room, but it didn't bother me because I was in no mood to talk. I heard Allison tell Chloe Dr. Goldman would probably order blood pressure medicine for me, do a pelvic exam, and possibly another ultrasound. I was trying my best not to worry, but at this point with my pregnancy being on the line and the new development of Shawn's wife, I wasn't sure how much more I could endure.

I had never been so glad to hear Dr. Goldman's voice as I did at that moment. "Hope," he exclaimed, "I just saw you yesterday and everything was fine. What in the world happened when you left my office?" He asked and I could tell he was genuinely concerned.

As I relayed the story of the burned lasagna, the smoke alarm, the chair and the fall, I realized how crazy I must sound to my doctor. But if he did think I was crazy he never let on. He told me everything that he was going to do which was everything Allison told Chloe.

But when he started talking to me again, that's when the anxiety set in. "The deciding factor in how we proceed with your care is the ultrasound. I reviewed your ultrasound images from last night and I am concerned about your cervix. I want to take another look, that will help me decide what will be best." I never heard him be so serious before and that made me a little nervous.

"Allison will get you some blood pressure medicine and something for pain. I'll have the ultrasound done right here and possibly a pelvic exam. I don't want you moving around if you don't have to," Dr. Goldman said as he stood up to leave the room. I watched as he left my room and sent up a silent prayer for strength.

True to Dr. Goldman's word, Allison was back in a few short minutes with medicine that she said would help start to regulate my blood pressure and some IV medicine for pain. Just as I was starting to doze off, the ultrasound tech came in pushing an ultrasound machine and Dr. Goldman was right behind her. He washed his hands at the sink by the door and Allison gave him a pair of gloves. He told me he would do the pelvic exam first.

I closed my eyes while I waited for him to be done. Once the ultrasound tech began the ultrasound, I was relieved to hear my baby's heartbeat, that sound alone gave me much needed reassurance. The ultrasound tech and Allison left my room leaving Dr. Goldman to speak with me. Chloe came over and stood by my bed so that she could hold my hand.

Dr. Goldman gave me a sympathetic look before he began to tell me the fate of my unborn child. You have a chance to carry this baby to term, but it's going to require some work on both our parts. Your cervix is measuring short, and it's way too early for that, I need to perform a surgical procedure to sew up your cervix that's called a cerclage. The success rate for women carrying their babies to term after a cerclage is very high. However we can't do it for two more weeks, you have to be at least twelve weeks in order for me to do the procedure. Since you are only ten weeks, this will be your home for the next two weeks. I need to keep your blood pressure under control and keep you off of your feet. The next two weeks are crucial for your baby and we will do everything we can to make you as comfortable as possible."

Doubt began to creep its way back in my mind as I tried to digest everything I was just told. I could not believe I was going through all of this.

Hearing the voicemail left from Shawn's wife, and now hearing that I was stuck in the hospital for the next two weeks was devastating. Not to mention, at some point I had to tell Shawn about the pregnancy. As if I wasn't nervous about it before, I was definitely nervous now with his wife all of a sudden making an appearance. My thoughts were interrupted when Dr. Goldman asked if I had any questions for him. You would think I had a million questions, but I honestly didn't. All I wanted to do was close my eyes and pretend this was all a bad dream.

CHAPTER 7

Not only did Ms. Claire come see me before she left the day I met her, but she had come to my room every day since then. She would even put in special orders for me when my cravings kicked in. I had been at the hospital for a week. After talking to Chloe, Tamera, and even Ms. Claire, we all felt it was best to wait to tell Shawn about the baby after the cerclage was placed. With my blood pressure still being up and down, mostly up, we all agreed that I could not handle the stress that may come along with my confession. I hadn't gotten any more calls from his wife and I was more than pleased about that. However Shawn had began texting me at least once a day asking me to call him or asking when we could talk. Part of me wanted to get this inevitable talk over with, but I wasn't prepared to deal with his wife.

It was one of the rare times when both Chloe and Tamera were in my room with me. I was sitting up in bed with my feet propped on two pillows.

Tamera was giving me an update on what was going on at the salon. It made me happy that between her and Sandra all of my clients could still get their hair done without going to another salon. We were all laughing because all of my clients refused to go to Leslie. Cassandra was trying to help her by letting her do some of my clients, but they were not having it. I felt good to laugh and not think about my current situation. Unfortunately that feeling didn't last long.

Chloe turned the volume all the way down on the TV and gave Tamera and me a look I couldn't figure out. "I need to tell you both something and I need you to let me finish before you say anything. This is really not easy for me." Chloe wiped a few tears from her eyes before she began to speak again. "I can't have children." Tamera and I exchanged glances and I'm sure both of us wanted to say something.

Chloe took a deep breath and began to tell us about one of the most tragic events of her life. "I know you guys remember five years ago when I was with Kevin and we moved in together. Well shortly after we moved in together, I found out that I was pregnant." At this point tears were freely flowing down Chloe's face, but she continued to talk. "I really wanted this baby, but Kevin didn't feel the same way. As soon as I told him he told me to have an abortion. We argued about it every day. He said we weren't ready to be parents and if I kept the baby there was no guarantee that he would be there to help me raise him or her. I didn't want to lose Kevin so I finally gave in and agreed to have an abortion. I was miserable and to make matters worse I was scared to tell anyone what was going on. I don't know why I wasn't strong enough to put my foot down and stand up for my baby."

I know this must have been hard for her to admit what she had gone through in secret. Chloe wiped her eyes as she continued. "I kept pushing my appointment back hoping that Kevin would have a change of heart. Then one day while I was getting ready for work, I started having really bad abdominal cramps, I started throwing up, and I had a low grade fever. Then my water broke, I didn't know it then, I didn't find out until I got the hospital. I drove myself to the emergency room, I didn't even call Kevin, I just went alone."

At this point, I was crying and so was Tamera. I never knew one of my closest friends had to carry such a heavy burden alone. I didn't understand why she didn't tell us, we knew everything about each other, or so I thought. Chloe looked at both of us with so much hurt in her eyes it was heartbreaking.

Even though I'm sure reliving this was not easy for her, she continued. "I didn't know how far along I was until that day at the hospital. I was already twenty weeks pregnant. I couldn't believe I was that far along, I hadn't gained much weight or anything. The ultrasound confirmed how far along I was and that I had very little amniotic fluid. I had an infection because my water broke, and apparently had been slowly leaking for a few days. They admitted me to the hospital and told me I would have to deliver my baby, and at twenty weeks the chance of survival was slim to none. Once I was in the room the doctor induced my labor, and eight hours later I delivered a little boy who lived for seven minutes. I got to hold him, he was perfect so tiny but perfect. I named him Gabriel because he was my angel. I called Kevin to ask him to come say goodbye to his son. He promised he'd be there, but never showed up. By the time I got home from the hospital, all of his things were out of the apartment."

Now things were starting to make since. The breakup between Chloe and Kevin had been really abrupt. All she told us was that they realized they wanted different things out of life. That is around the time Chloe started going to church and also the time she left the obstetrics and gynecology practice she was doing ultrasounds at and started working at the imaging center.

"Even though I just said a mouthful, there is more," Chloe said while wringing her hands pacing the floor. "I continued to bleed for a month straight after I delivered. I was always in pain so I finally went to my doctor who found out I had fibroids all over my uterus. My doctor decided the best option was to have a hysterectomy. All of my dreams of having a big family died in that moment. I felt like I was being punished for even considering having an abortion, but once I really got to know God I understood that what we go through is not for us, but to help someone else in their time of need."

Chloe walked over to my bed and gave me a hug, Tamera joined us. We just hugged and cried for what felt like hours.

"I actually feel better, like a weight has lifted," Chloe said when we released our hug.

Tamera gave Chloe a stern look, but she spoke with love. "We are more than friends we are sisters. Please don't ever allow yourself to go through anything alone again. I love y'all and will do anything for both of you."

Chloe was the next one to speak. "Hope, I am going to do everything I can to help you carry this baby full term. I don't want you to stress about anything, you have us right by your side."

I already knew that, but it still felt good to hear. But it was something weighing on my mind and I had to ask. "Is this why you left your ultrasound job at the doctor's office?"

Chloe nodded her head before she spoke. "It is, I just couldn't take seeing all those pregnant women and taking images of their unborn babies. When I found out I couldn't have any more children that put me over the edge. I had to fight tears every time I had to perform an ultrasound, which was several times a day. When I saw there was an opening at the imaging center, I jumped on the opportunity."

Hearing everything Chloe went through gave me a new perspective on my pregnancy. All though I was only at eleven weeks, I have a good chance of making it through to the end. I have excellent medical care and an awesome support team. At that moment I realized my support team needed to a few more players, my parents.

CHAPTER 8

We made it to week twelve. It wasn't easy, but we made it. My blood pressure continued to fluctuate between normal and high, which is the reason I kept getting headaches according to my doctor. The bleeding eventually slowed down, but I did experience spotting along with some pretty painful cramping. Dr. Goldman and all the different nurse's I'd met over the past two weeks were wonderful. Some days Bianca and Allison would just check in with me even if they weren't assigned to my room.

Since I had lost all of my grandparents, I connected with Ms. Claire in a way I never thought possible. She prayed with and for me, encouraged me and made sure my pregnancy cravings were satisfied. Sometimes she would bring me food from home that she cooked, some of the best cooking I ever had. I was pretty sure this was against hospital policy but she'd always say she was doing the work of the Lord when I tried to protest.

It was the day before I was having my cerclage placed to keep my cervix closed. I was nervous about the procedure, but even more nervous about seeing my parents. I finally gathered enough courage to call them and tell them everything, even the part about Shawn being married. I just knew that my mom and dad would be disappointed in me and I was not prepared for them to be so accepting. They promised they would be in Charlotte the day before my procedure and were prepared to stay as long as they needed to. Both of my parents were retired so they had plenty of time on their hands. They moved from Charlotte when they retired because it had gotten too city, as they said, for them. My mom's parents were from a small town, St. George, South Carolina. When my grandmother passed away two years ago, she left the family house to my mom and dad. I was shocked my parents wanted to live in a town known for having a yearly grits festival.

I was flipping through the channels enjoying some peace and quiet when my parents walked into my room. I wanted to jump up and run into my father's arms.

"There's my baby girl," my dad yelled as he came over by my bed so he could give me a hug. It felt so good to be in the presence of my parents.

"Joseph, let me get a good look at my baby," my mom said as she put her purse on the couch.

She came over and gently pushed my dad out of the way. My mom hugged me and stepped back to look me directly in my eyes. She was absolutely beautiful if I say so myself. Standing at only five ft. three she still commanded attention when she walked into a room. We shared the same caramel complexion and she wore her salt and pepper hair in a boy short natural. My parents still looked good together after thirty-eight years together. My dad was the total opposite of my mom. He was six two with deep mahogany skin. He opted to keep a clean shaved head since he lost all of his hair in the top.

"Pumpkin," my mom said referring to me using my childhood nickname. "Why would you wait so long to inform us of what was going on? We would have been here much sooner."

My dad quickly intervened. "Now Val, we talked about this, no should haves or could haves, we are here now that is all that matters."

I smiled relieved that my dad saved me from one of my mom's famous lectures.

"Thank you, Daddy." I said as my dad kissed me on the forehead before taking a seat on the recliner across from my bed.

Hope's Faith   Raegan Dennis

My mom made me scoot over in my bed so she could sit down. I rested my head on her shoulder as she rubbed my head. This is something she used to do when I was sick as a little girl and it always put me to sleep.

However, I knew sleep was not going to happen with me being nervous about the procedure. I still closed my eyes and silently thanked God my parents were here. Now that they were here, I couldn't figure out why I waited so long to tell them. My mom was a little harder on me than my dad, but he was always able to talk her into seeing my side of things as well as her own point of view. Needless to say I usually went to my dad first for that exact reason.

I remembered when I first figured out I wanted to be a hairstylist. It was always in the back of my mind, but when we had a career day when I was a junior in high school my mind was made up. I came home from school so excited to tell my parents that I knew what I wanted to do once I graduated from high school. Of course I beat both of them home. My mom was an insurance underwriter and my dad was the general manager for a chain of grocery stores. My mom usually got home at five thirty on the dot. My dad's arrival time varied depending on which store he was stationed at for the day.

I decided to cook dinner so we wouldn't have to wait for mom to cook and I could tell them my good news. I made baked chicken, rice pilaf and asparagus. I already had three plates made along with iced tea. My dad arrived home first and was impressed that I took the initiative to cook. My mom was a little later than usual and when she walked in I could see the frustration all over her face. She told us it was a terrible accident on interstate eighty five and she sat still for thirty minutes in traffic. I thought that maybe this wasn't the best day to tell them with my mom being in bad mood and I knew her heart was set on me going to a four year college.

As we sat down to eat dinner, my dad blessed the food as he always did. My mom thanked me for cooking and I thought it was a good time to break the news. I told them about career day and how I always had an interest in doing hair and there were a few different cosmetology schools in Charlotte I could choose from. My mom put her fork down and told me I would go to a traditional four year college so I could have a real career and there was nothing to discuss. She put her fork down and got up from the table. My dad patted my hand and assured me that he would talk to her and if this was my dream he would make sure it happened.

I was brought back to the present time when my mom asked when the girls would be there. No matter how old we got my parents still referred to us as the girls. Once they met Chloe and a few years later met Tamera, they instantly became a part of our family.

"They will be here tomorrow, they wanted to give us some time together," I told my mom as I sat up.

"I was looking forward to seeing my babies" my mom said poking her bottom lip out.

My dad looked up from the news he had been watching. "We will have plenty of time to see the girls, we are in no rush to get back to St. George. Depending on what the doctor is saying we will stay as long as we need to."

I didn't know how I felt about having long-term house guests. Especially my own parents. The bright side was they were excellent cooks, I wouldn't have to worry about cleaning, or laundry, or driving for that matter. The downside was I would have absolutely no privacy and my dad would watch the news all day if he could. I always thought the news was so negative so I rarely watched it. But my dad was always saying he had to stay informed. But I knew this wasn't the time to worry about something that may or may not happen.

"Pumpkin, I don't mean to stress you or bring up any bad memories, but when do you plan on telling this young man about his baby?" My mom asked.

Before I could even respond, my dad gave my mother a look I couldn't decipher. "Valerie, let's get through tomorrow and we will tackle everything else once we know our first grandchild is out of harm's way," he said.

I was so grateful for my father standing up for me. I knew what I had to do as far as Shawn was concerned, but my main priority was keeping my baby safe, that meant me not stressing myself out.

After a few hours of watching CNN news, my dad got up and asked my mom if she was ready to go back to their hotel.

"We need to let Hope rest and I am starving," my mom answered my dad while gathering her things.

My dad got up and walked over to my bed and gave me a hug. "What time do we need to be here in the morning?" He asked still holding onto me like I was a little girl.

"Dr. Goldman said they would prep me at five in the morning," I answered my dad as I broke free from our embrace.

My mom was the next to speak. "Well, that means we need to be here by four thirty. We need to pray for you and make sure you are covered before you go down." She came over and gave me a hug and a peck on the cheek. "We love you pumpkin and get some rest." She said as they walked out of my room.

CHAPTER 9

Glory be to God that I was released from the hospital two days after my cervix was sewn up. I had strict orders from Dr. Goldman that I was to remain on bedrest for the remainder of my pregnancy. I also had to see a high risk obstetrician every week to measure my cervix and check my blood pressure. As long as everything went well I would get the cerclage removed at thirty four or thirty five weeks. Dr. Goldman had a long talk with me before I left the hospital. The goal was to keep me pregnant as long as possible. He wanted me to understand each week that I carried my baby the better chance of survival he or she had. A new milestone was met each week, so the longer my baby got to bake the better their health would be once I delivered.

I honestly wasn't prepared to be out of work for the next seven months, not to mention the eight weeks I was taking after I gave birth. I needed to talk to Cassandra and give her my doctor's note. One of the things I loved about working at Studio Seven salon was that Cassandra was very compassionate. I was independent which meant I rented a booth from her. In other situations like mine you were expected to pay your booth rent even when you were unable to work. Cassandra did not operate that way. Her philosophy was if you wanted to keep good stylist, treat your stylist like they are good stylist. If you had documentation of why you were not able to work she would hold your station without charging you any booth rent while you were out.

Cassandra agreed to come by my apartment so I wouldn't put the baby at risk. I knew one of my parents would have taken me to the salon but Cassandra reminded me that I was on complete bedrest. It was still early in the day and I knew I needed to look at my checking and savings accounts. I took my laptop off my nightstand and logged onto my online banking. I probably had enough to keep everything up for the next three or four months. That was not nearly enough when I was looking at about nine months out of work. The stress that everyone was warning me about was about to overtake me. There was nothing I could do about my financial situation at that moment so I logged off, put my laptop up and took a nap.

I woke up a few hours later to the sound of talking and laughing coming from my living room. I went to the bathroom to take a look in the mirror to make sure I was presentable. Other than my hair being in desperate need of some attention I wasn't too bad looking considering what I was going through. I would let Tamera do something to my hair eventually but for now I wouldn't worry about it.

I came out of my bedroom and walked down the short hall that led to the living room. Cassandra jumped up and gave me a tight squeeze. She looked stunning as she always did. Her naturally curly hair was fire engine red, which complimented her light brown skin. Her hazel eyes gave her a mysterious beauty. She was dressed down in a black fitted T-shirt that had the Studio Seven logo on the front and address on the back paired with fitted Blue Jeans and black and white Converse.

"It is so good lay my eyes on you, I've been praying for you and the baby," she said as she sat back down.

" I'm so glad my baby works for a good God fearing woman like you," My mom said coming out of the kitchen.

She sat a pound cake on the bar that separated the kitchen and the living room. Since my mom retired from insurance she was in one of two places, the kitchen or her garden. Since I didn't have a garden to tend to I assumed she would be spending much of her time in the kitchen.

"Mom, you didn't have to bake a cake," I said, I didn't want her thinking she had to do anything special for my company.

"Speak for yourself Hope, I appreciate a homemade cake any day," Cassandra said as my mom handed her a slice of cake.

She and my mom talked small talk while attempted to get up to go get my doctor's note.

My mom quickly got up and began fussing. "Hope, bedrest is just that, bedrest, no unnecessary moving around. What do you need, I'll get it for you."

Feeling like a scolded child I just sat on my tan colored library and crossed my arms over my chest. "I was getting my doctor's note for Cassandra mom," I said with a little too much attitude in my voice.

"I'm still the mother little girl," she said while making her way down the hallway to my room.

My mom returned to the living room with the folder I got from the hospital when I was discharged. She rummaged through a the papers until she came across the note stating I was to remain on bedrest until I delivered my baby.

"I'll make a copy and have Tamera bring you the original back, you will need that," Cassandra said taking the paper from my mom.

"What do you mean I'll need it?" I asked a little confused. I always kept my original copies of paperwork, but that was because that was one of the life skills my mom instilled in me.

"You will need it to file for your long-term disability," Cassandra said matter-of-factly.

Now I was really confused. "Cassandra what are you talking about, I'm not sure I'm following you," I said trying to recall what she could be talking about.

"Do you remember when one of my clients did a presentation for the salon a few years ago about long term and short term disability? You, I and Tamera all signed up for it and we agreed that I would raise your booth rent just enough to cover your premium and I would pay it for all three of us," Cassandra said jogging my memory. She pulled out a manila envelope with my name on it. I opened it and started reading, which was useless because it made no sense to me. My mom walked over and put on the reading glasses that had been top of her head.

"Let me see that, I can tell you don't know what in the world you are reading," my mom said making me feel like a child for the second time. My mom scanned over the documents then looked at me then Cassandra. A smile slowly spread across her face.

"What mom, tell me," I said the impatience evident in my voice.

My mom took her reading glasses off and placed them on the coffee table before she explained. "You have a long term disability policy which means you will get sixty percent of your income while you are out of work on bed rest."

I felt like the weight of the world had just lifted off my shoulders. Cassandra nor my mom knew that I was just looking at my finances wondering how I was going to make it. I began to cry tears of joy as I told them how that very day I was wondering what I was going to do because I only had enough to keep things going for three maybe four months. My mom got up and started doing her holy ghost dance all over my living room.

I really forgot we signed up for long term disability, I never thought about it or thought I'd need it. I was so glad to have Cassandra as a leader. She always thought for the future and tried her best to help us do the same. I believe that's why we were a successful salon.

Once my mom finished praising the Lord, it was back to business. Her glasses were back on and she had even found a highlighter. I could tell she was really in her element. She had moved from the living room to my small dining table placed in the area designated for a dining room table beside the kitchen. You couldn't call it a dining room because it was much too small.

"Okay ladies, this is what we have," she said while looking over her glasses at me and Cassandra. "Since you are self-employed you have to submit your last year tax return along with your doctor's note stating that you are on bed rest. They will then verify with your doctor that you are unable to work and why you are unable to work. They will use your tax return to determine what your average take home pay is. Your payments will be sixty percent of your average. You will receive a deposit in your checking account once a month. You can actually file immediately, there is normally a two week waiting period before you can file but you have surpassed that at this point."

I don't know how my mom made that sound so simple, but she did. Even though it was sixty percent of what I averaged, I was okay with that because I made good money at the salon. I wouldn't even have to touch what I had in my savings account. Cassandra told my mom she could come by the salon to fax the paperwork to the insurance company tomorrow. My mom hugged Cassandra and told her how much better she felt knowing that she looked out for the best interest of her hairstylist.

"Mrs. Val that is how I've been in business for so long, I'm blessed to be a blessing," Cassandra told my mom. I hugged Cassandra and she promised to come by and check on me soon before she left.

CHAPTER 10

My pregnancy was progressing and I finally felt like my baby was out of the danger zone. I was at fifteen weeks and I was able I to find out if I was having a girl or a boy at my next appointment. My mom had practically moved into my apartment and my dad went back and forth between Charlotte and St. George. He wanted to keep an eye on the house and make sure the grass stayed cut. I really did love my parents and I was thankful that they altered their life to make sure I was being taken care of.

But sometimes I longed for an empty apartment and to just be by myself. Even when my mom would go grocery shopping and bring a different brand of an item than I would buy started to irritate me. I had been craving orange juice so my mom said she would run to the store and get some for me. I felt like my mouth was watering the whole time I was waiting on her to get back. As soon as she walked in the front door, I got up from where I was laying on the sofa.

"Bed rest young lady," my mom said, but not before I saw the orange juice that she bought.

"Mom," I said in the most annoyed voice I could muster up. "It has to be Tropicana, not Minute Maid."

My mom put the glass down that she had just pulled from the cabinet and gave me a look only a mother could give. "You got what was on sale, be grateful. I'm going to let you have a pass this time and assume it's your hormones that would make you react that way. Next time I don't mind putting you and your hormones in check."

I took the glass she held out for me and made my way back to the sofa. I was scrolling through my phone as I drank my orange juice, which wasn't half bad, but I wouldn't let my mom know that. I returned a few text messages and began playing a game when my phone alerted me that I had another text message.

Hope, please call me I've been trying to contact you for weeks now. We need to talk soon.

I put my phone back on the coffee table and picked up the remote. I don't know why I thought the TV would be a distraction. I flipped through a few channels hoping to find something to watch. My mom came out of the kitchen wiping her hands on a dish towel. She sat down beside me and put the dish towel on the coffee table. We sat and watched TV in silence for a few minutes. I sat up so I could look at my mom.

"He sent me a text," I said before I lost the nerve.

"Who, pumpkin?" My mom asked while laughing at something on TV.

"Shawn, the father of my baby, just texted me. I really don't want to talk to him. Can't I just keep my baby to myself? Do I really have to tell him?" I started crying just at the thought of my baby being around his wife.

My mom grabbed my hand before she spoke. "I can't imagine how hard this is for you. You are so courageous to take on being a mother knowing the father may or may not be around. But you know what the right thing to do is."

I knew what the right thing to do was, I just didn't want to do the right thing. Shawn didn't do the right thing with me.

"Vengeance is mine." I heard the voice of the Lord loud and clear.

I was wondering if my mom heard the same thing as I did, because what she said next was only confirmation.

"Pumpkin, that is not how we as children of God act. It's not your place to punish him. I'm sure the Lord is already dealing with him. That may be why he keeps trying to get in touch with you. Be the bigger person. Tell him about his child," she said still holding my hand.

Just as I was thinking that this lecture wasn't so bad, she continued. "You don't want your child to resent you because he or she doesn't have a relationship with their dad. Look at all the favor God has already shown you with this baby."

Once again the floodgates of tears started as I continued to listen to my mom. "Things were not looking so good for the baby just a few short weeks ago, threatening a miscarriage but God saw you through. Not to mention the long term disability that you forgot that you had, now you can rest easy knowing you are financially stable while you are out of work."

I couldn't deny how blessed I was at that moment. Everything thus far had worked out in my favor. Why couldn't I trust God with this situation.

My mom wiped the tears from my face then held onto both of my hands as she continued. "I know God has got this worked out, the Lord isn't looking down at you trying to figure out what to do, or shocked that you are pregnant. He knows just what will happen and exactly when it needs to happen."

Listening to my mom was starting to give me the confidence I needed to confront Shawn, until I heard the next thing my mom said.

"Lord knows I wish you would have waited until you were married to have a baby, but at the rate you are going that may have never happened I should just be grateful that I'm even having a grandbaby, I was starting to lose hope."

Now that was the mom that I knew. The slight tone of judgement and disapproval in her voice. Not quite accepting me for me in private but the doting mother in public. I was pretty positive that she waited until my father wasn't around to defend me to tell me how she really felt. He would always stand up for me when me and my mom didn't see eye to eye. I released my hands from hers and stood up. I was making my way down the hall to get to my bedroom. I stopped when I was halfway down the hall and turned around. I was not a little girl, I could tell her how I felt without fear of reprimand. Once I got in front of my mom who was still sitting on the sofa, I said what I needed to say. I didn't even bother sitting down because I was going to make it short and to the point.

"Mom, I'm already beating myself up about this. Please don't get in the ring with me. Can you stand on the sideline and cheer me on, for once?" With that said, I made my way back down the hall to my bedroom and slept until the next day

CHAPTER 11

I was really excited that it was time for me to find out if I was having a boy or a girl. My mom had not brought up our disagreement and neither had I. My dad had come back so he could be with me for the ultrasound. I know he felt the tension brewing in my small apartment because he kept asking my mom did anything interesting happen while he was in St. George. The only answer my dad would get was my mom telling him to ask his daughter.

I was looking for some clothes that actually fit my growing belly so I could get dressed for my appointment. I made a mental note to go online and order a few things. If my stomach was this big at four months, I could only imagine how big I'd be in the months to come. Just as I was pulling on a pair of black leggings and a black and white striped shirt that was on the borderline of being too tight, my doorbell rang.

"Is Hope here?" There is no way I heard what I thought I heard. My heart began to beat rapidly and I could almost feel my blood pressure rising. I took a look in the mirror to make sure I looked presentable. My pixie cut had grown out tremendously and I was wearing a short wrap. Before I could make my way out of my bedroom, my mom came in and closed the door.

"Hope, Shawn is standing in your living room. I kept telling you to call him and tell him," my mom said. How do you think he is going to react to seeing you this way and he knows absolutely nothing?" Leave it to my mom to say I told you so. I honestly didn't think he would just show up.

"Mom, please, can we not do this right now?" I said trying to control my frustration.

Of course she kept going in true Valerie Daniels fashion. "You are about to be a mother young lady and your child will need a father. Your father can't fix this one for you, you did this, now get out there and talk to that man so we don't miss your appointment."

I finally made it out of my bedroom and down the short hallway to the living room. Shawn was sitting on my loveseat talking to my parents. I didn't want to admit it, but he looked as good as he did since I last saw him almost six months ago. He looked like he just left the barbershop, his low haircut was full of waves and his goatee was trimmed to perfection. He stood up and I to look up to admire the sight before me. Standing six feet three inches he towered over me, he looked more like a football player than a computer geek. He taught computer technology at East Mecklenburg high school. His hazel eyes and light brown skin is what got me in trouble in the first place. I should not be attracted to this married man, but I was. I didn't think these feelings would resurface, I thought I was over him. Maybe that was the real reason I wasn't in a rush to tell him about his child. My thoughts were interrupted when Shawn reached out and touched my stomach.

"It looks like we need to talk," he said as he made small circles with his index finger on my stomach.

I stepped back as a signal for him to stop. It was little things like that that broke me down in the first place. I wish I could say I didn't like it, but that would not be true.

I looked up into his hazel eyes as I spoke. "We have quite a few things to discuss, but right now is not the best time."

Shawn grabbed my hand and I pulled it back, I think more for effect than anything.

"I'm ninety-nine percent sure that is my baby you're carrying, why would you not tell me. It's not like I haven't been trying to get in contact with you," he said while staring at my protruding stomach.

Now it was my turn to be upset. "Maybe I didn't tell you I was pregnant for the same reason you didn't tell me you were married." I knew I was being petty, but at that moment I didn't want to be the bigger person.

Shawn sat back down on the loveseat and ran his hand over his face. "Hope, he said sounding defeated, that's why I've been calling you, part of the reason anyway, but you wouldn't answer your phone or respond to my text messages. I took a huge chance by popping up, but I'm glad I did. I may have never knew about my child."

My dad interrupted our reunion. " Hope, Val we probably better get moving, we don't want to be late for your appointment."

Before I could ask Shawn if we could sit down and talk later, my mom spoke up. "Look at God, it's such a blessing you stopped by today Shawn. Why don't you come to the doctor with us? We find out what Hope is having today."

If I thought my blood pressure was rising before, I knew for a fact it was rising now. I couldn't believe my mom invited him to my ultrasound. Just as I was thinking it didn't matter because I was sure Shawn would say no he stood up and pulled his car keys out of his pocket. "I'll drive," he said and headed for the door.

Once we made it outside, Shawn opened the passenger door of his black Nissan Armada for me. I climbed into the seat and put on my seatbelt.

The smell of his favorite cologne Burberry Touch, mixed with the car air freshener brought back a flood of memories. Our first date, sitting in his car talking for hours because neither of us wanted to end the night, our first kiss, these were just a few things that came to my mind. I wondered if he was having similar thoughts because of the way he looked at me and winked. He closed the passenger door and made his way to the back door to open it for my mom and help her into the backseat.

"Aren't you quite the gentleman," my mom said as she looked around Shawn's SUV. I should have known she wouldn't end there. "There is certainly enough room for a car seat and a stroller too, for that matter."

I looked in the backseat so I could give my mom a warning look, but with my dad being there it wasn't necessary.

"Val, don't start with these young people, they have enough to figure out without you making a big fuss." My dad gave my mom a look that we both knew well, the look that meant the discussion was over.

My blood pressure was slightly elevated, but with the morning I had I wasn't surprised. The first part of my ultrasound was done without anyone else in my room. Dr. Goldman needed to check my cervix to make sure there were no major changes that we needed to be concerned about.

Once he saw that everything looked good, he sent his nurse, Stacey, to get my parents and Shawn so they could witness the second part of my ultrasound.

While we waited on everyone to come to the exam room, Dr. Goldman took the opportunity to talk to me about my progress. "Hope, I still need you to take it easy, things are looking better but we are not quite out of the woods. In high risk pregnancies, the goal is to get you to twenty-seven weeks. Obviously, we want you to make it longer than that, but at twenty-seven weeks if you were to deliver chances of survival are good, but get better with each week." I made it this far so I had to trust God that would see me through.

The image on the screen was absolutely breathtaking. Dr. Goldman was pointing out various body parts while my parents and Shawn looked on in amazement.

"Do we want to know what we are having?" Dr. Goldman asked while studying the image on the screen.

"Yes," we all said in unison.

"It looks like you will be decorating in pink, it's a girl," Dr. Goldman said as he printed out a few pictures. "Remember Hope, off of your feet and remember to take your blood pressure medicine every day. I'll see you next week," Dr. Goldman said as he walked out of the exam room.

CHAPTER 12

The ride back to my apartment was quiet. Jazz flowed out of the car speakers. I'm sure Shawn chose to listen to Jazz for the benefit of my parents, which was actually very thoughtful of him. Since the cat was out of the bag, I had no choice than to talk to him about his level of participation in our daughter's life. I had quite a few questions about his wife and how she would play into this scenario. I know that Shawn was her dad, but I refused to have my child around a woman scorned.

When we arrived back at my apartment, my dad was the first to speak. "Val, I need to run to the grocery store, come ride with me."

My dad patted me on the shoulder and when I looked back he gave me a wink. I knew he was giving me and Shawn the opportunity to talk privately without my mother's input. I thanked God for that small miracle.

As my parents walked across the parking lot to get into my mom's Toyota Camry, Shawn helped me out of his car and up the one flight of steps that led to my apartment. Once we made our way inside I had a seat on the sofa and Shawn sat on the loveseat.

"Hope, I came by to apologize and explain some things to you, but it looks like we both have some explaining to do," he said as he got up and sat beside me.

"You go first," I said trying to buy a little more time.

"First of all, let me apologize for the way things ended between us, or should I say the way I ended things." Shawn actually sounded sincere. "You did not deserve what I did. You are beautiful, ambitious, intelligent, independent and I admire all of those things about you. When I broke up with you, I thought I was protecting you."

Now I was really confused. "How would hurting me protect me Shawn?" I knew there was a hint of attitude in my voice but I could care less. I really wanted to know about his wife but instead of asking I decided to hear him out hoping he would answer my unasked questions.

"I got married really young, fresh out of college. Both of our parents tried to warn us that we were too young, but when you are in love, you never hear what anyone else has to say." Shawn moved a little closer to me on the sofa before he continued. It didn't take long for us to realize we were completely incompatible. I wanted a house full of kids, she didn't. We could never agree on television shows or movies. I'd be in one room watching one thing and she would be in another room watching something else. If I stayed late at the high school to tutor some of the kids I must have been out with another woman. We eventually turned into roommates, literal roommates, sleeping in two separate rooms. One day I came home later than normal because it was the homecoming football game and the principals like all the staff to stay for those types of events. I got home about ten o'clock that night." He stood up and started pacing the floor back and forth. I could see that whatever happened could not have been easy for him to tell me, but he continued.

"When I walked in the door of our home, it was empty. She had taken everything we owned. All that was left was my clothes, my personal belongings and my computer. I knew we had been arguing a lot more than usual, but I never thought Alana would leave, just up and leave and take everything. I tried my best to sleep that night but it was impossible. I started thinking, if she took everything out of the house, what about the money we had been saving to buy a house? I logged into my online banking and saw that my personal account had not been touched, but the joint account was empty."

Shawn finally sat back down, but he was far from finished. "Alana's mom called me a few days later to inform me Alana had met someone else and was moving out of state and I could send any divorce documentation to her mother. Her mom kept apologizing for her daughter. She told me she tried to get her to do things the right way. When I asked why Alana would just up and leave and take everything without so much as a note, her mom just sighed and said she asked her the same thing, all she said was she just didn't love me anymore."

Shawn rubbed his hands over his face, I notice that was something he did when he was anxious about something.

"I waited the year that North Carolina requires before you can file for divorce. I had the papers delivered to her mom's house. That is around the same time I met you. When I saw you walking out of the mall, something in me came back to life. I wasn't going to approach you, but I knew if I didn't I'd regret it for the rest of my life."

I remember that day like it was yesterday, the attraction was mutual and when he walked up to me the butterflies in my stomach took flight. Shawn and I shared a smile as we both remembered that day.

"Hope, I was planning on being divorced before things turned serious, I thought I was practically divorced when I met you," he said as he kept his hazel eyed gaze on me. "When we slept together and you told me you couldn't continue because of your relationship with God, I just used that as an excuse to break up with you. I felt like I could get my divorce finalized and hopefully you would forgive me for breaking up with you the way I did. I planned on explaining everything to you, but Alana was refusing to sign the divorce papers prolonging me moving on with my life.

When you called me and we had the conversation about your celibacy, Alana showed up at my house saying she made a big mistake. The guy she left me for turned out to be abusive. I felt bad for her, but she made her choice and I made mine, my choice was you. When I told her that I was in a relationship she went ballistic saying that she was still my wife and she would make sure no other woman got close to me."

I was now beginning to understand the voicemail I got from his wife while I was in the hospital.

"Oh my God, Shawn, she left me a voicemail while I was in the hospital," I told him as the pieces to this puzzle were starting to connect.

He gave me a worried look as I reached on the coffee table and picked up my phone. I went through my voicemail until I found the message I was looking for. I handed Shawn my cellphone and watched him as he listened. I couldn't read his facial expression, but I could tell he was not happy.

"Hope, I'm so sorry. I never thought she would call you, I honestly thought that was an empty threat she made, she must have gone through my phone, but I don't know when that could have happened, other than the day she showed up at my house I haven't been around her." Then he snapped like a lightbulb went off. "It must have been when I went to her mom's house to ask about the divorce papers, we were sitting at the kitchen table and I got up to use the bathroom, I left my phone on the table. When I came back to the table she had ripped up divorce papers, now it makes sense." Shawn was back up pacing again. "Hope, I am getting a divorce, I talked to my lawyer yesterday. He said even if Alana doesn't sign the divorce papers the judge will still grant the divorce. This is the third attempt at getting her to sign them, if she doesn't the judge will grant my divorce if she doesn't respond within thirty days."

I wasn't sure how I felt at the moment. It was a lot of information to process. The fact still remained that Shawn did hurt me. I opened myself up to the possibility of love and he crushed my heart. Even with everything he just told me, those same butterflies from the day we met were still in my stomach.

By the time I gave Shawn all the details of my pregnancy, the miscarriage scare and my hospital stay, he was speechless. He reached over and began to rub my baby bump.

"If I had handled this differently, I could have been right by your side. I just don't understand why you didn't tell me about the baby. Let me ask you this, and be one hundred percent honest with me," Shawn said while rubbing my stomach.

I was pretty sure I knew what he was about to ask me. "If I didn't just happen to come by today, would you have even told me about our baby? I know I didn't handle things well with you and I will always regret that."

It was a fair question and I really had no reason to not tell him about the baby, just my own selfish reasons. I was still hurt and angry at him for the way he broke up with me.

"I had intentions of telling you the night I fell. I even made Chloe and Tamera come by so when I called you I wouldn't back out. But everything happened so fast. Then there was a chance that I would lose the baby, and then the phone call from your wife, I just kept putting it off. Now that I'm saying it out loud, it just sounds like a bunch of excuses. I should be apologizing to you." I looked down at my swollen feet, to avoid looking at Shawn.

He lifted my chin so I had no choice but to look him in the eye when he spoke. "We have both made some mistakes and we have both apologized, so where do we go from here?" That was a loaded question that I wasn't prepared to answer.

CHAPTER 13

I hadn't spent any time with my girls lately so I was excited when Tamera called to tell me they were coming by to spend the day with me and give my parents a break. It was a Saturday and I wasn't sure how Tamera was able to get out of the salon early, but I was happy she did. I was past the point of cabin fever so any company was welcome. I was lying on my sofa watching TV when there was a knock at the door. My mom came out of the kitchen to answer the door.

"Hello girls," my mom greeted Tamera and Chloe as she gave them both a hug. "I'm so glad you girls could come by, I'm sure I'm driving Hope crazy by now," my mom said. She didn't know how right she was. But since Shawn's visit she had actually been much better, so we had been getting along. I just hoped it stayed that way.

"Come on Val, let's get out of here," my dad yelled out while he made his way from the back of my apartment. "Now you two take care of my princesses," my dad said referring to me and my baby. I loved how protective my dad had always been over me and I couldn't help but wonder if Shawn would be this way with our daughter. Once my parents were gone Tamera and Chloe started hounding me for information.

"What makes you think you can send a text about Shawn with no details?" I should have known Tamera would have been the first to attack.

But Chloe was right behind her. "Right, when I read the text saying you talked to Shawn, I was waiting for another text with the rundown, but that never came."

I had to defend myself before they said anything else. "First of all, it was way too much to text and this is an in-person story."

Tamera sucked her teeth and threw a throw pillow at me. "Are you trying to hint at something?" She said trying not to laugh.

"Well it got y'all over here, it took a few weeks, but it got y'all over here," I said as I threw the pillow back at Tamera.

"Hold on," Chloe piped in, "some of us have to work, everyone doesn't get to lie around and have their mom take care of them."

Tamera stood up and put her hands on her hips before she started in on me. "As I recall not only am I doing my clients but I'm doing a lot of your clients as well, so excuse me for not coming by sooner, but I'm not mad at making money honey." We all got a good laugh at that. I was so happy to be with my two best friends. I finally told them about Shawn's surprise visit and my mom inviting him to my ultrasound appointment.

"I can't believe Mrs. Val did that," Chloe said looking at me in disbelief.

Tamera looked at Chloe and started laughing. "I don't know why you can't believe it, I sure can, you know how Mrs. Val is. But the important thing is that Shawn actually went to the appointment and it sounds like he will be an active part of my niece's life," she said.

Knowing that Shawn was going to be there for our daughter gave me mixed feelings. One part of me was happy and relieved that I wouldn't be a completely single parent, but the other part of me didn't know how I would handle being around him on a regular basis.

Of course I had to fill my best friends in on the drama with Shawn's soon to be ex-wife and his strange logic behind our breakup.

"I wouldn't worry about her, you know how women are these days.

By the time the baby is born, she won't be thinking about him," Chloe said before she got up to go to the kitchen.

I didn't want to worry about Alana, but I did. I hadn't gotten any other phone calls from her outside of the one, so Chloe was probably right.

"So, what do you think is going to happen with you and Shawn once his divorce is final?"

Tamera asked me. She and Chloe both looked at me waiting on my answer. I wish I knew the answer myself.

"I don't know, I honestly don't know," I said sitting up.

"Let me rephrase that, what do you want to happen?" Tamera asked as she got off the floor where she had been sitting and sat beside me on the couch.

I thought about it for a few seconds before I answered. I was rubbing my growing belly thinking of how I felt when Shawn rubbed in the same spot. "I wish we could start over. Seeing him brought back so many feelings that I thought were gone. But I can't think of any of that until his divorce is final."

"When is the last time you saw Shawn?" Chloe asked.

"Well," I said, I asked him to give me some time to process things, so I haven't seen him, but he calls and texts me every day to check on me and our baby girl. The more we communicate the, the more I want things to work out between us. But how can I trust him after he kept his marriage from me? Not to mention how he broke up with me."

The pregnancy hormones were getting the best of me and I was doing my best to hold back the tears that were threatening to fall.

. Chloe was sitting on one side of me and Tamera was on the other side. Chloe held my hand while I surrendered to the tears and allowed them to fall.

Tamera turned so she could face me as she spoke. "Look Hope, I know this isn't easy and you don't have to make a decision today. But let's just look at the facts. Shawn did admit he was wrong and he did apologize. Let's not forget how consistent he was trying to get in contact with you."

Chloe looked at me and smirked as she gave her input. "Let's not forget that you avoided the man so bad he had to show up on your doorstep unannounced. I was beginning to wonder if you were going to tell him about the baby. So you were in the wrong too, you should not have waited that long to tell him."

Leave it to real friends to tell the truth, even if it wasn't what you wanted to hear. That was one of the many things I loved about our friendship, we said what needed to be said and there were never any hard feelings. I wiped my face and turned to face one of my best friends then the other.

"I don't know what I would do without you two," I said as more tears fell.

"Okay, enough with the tears," Tamera said as she got up from the sofa to make her way to the kitchen, we need to feed you and our niece.

We watched movies, ate Chinese food and laughed all night until we all fell asleep. Chloe was asleep on the loveseat and Tamera had fallen asleep on the floor. My baby was resting on my bladder so I had to get up to make it to the bathroom. The bigger I got, the more trips to the bathroom I had to take. Once I made it back to the sofa, I saw the light on my cell phone blinking. My mom had called to let me know they went to check on the house in St. George and they would be back the next day. Shawn had called but didn't leave a voicemail but he did text me.

I just wanted to check on you and our baby girl. I know you said you needed time, but I hope to see you soon. Call me!

I checked the time to see if it was too late to call Shawn back. It was one thirty in the morning so I decided to text him, if he was sleep hopefully that would be less of a chance of waking him up.

Are you up?

Before I could put the phone down, it alerted me that I had a text message.

Yes. Do you feel like talking?

Instead of replying to his last text message, I decided to call. I waddled down the hall to my bedroom so I could talk without waking up Chloe and Tamera. I got as comfortable as I could in my queen sized bed. I found Shawn's name and hit the talk button. I put the phone to my ear and he answered on the first ring as if he was anticipating my call.

"Shouldn't you be resting?" He asked concern evident in his voice.

"Hello to you too," I said.

"Seriously, why aren't you asleep? I called you hours ago, I just figured you had gone to bed already," he questioned me.

The sound of his voice was mesmerizing and it took me a minute to gather my thoughts.

"I was asleep, but I had to use the bathroom, and when I got up I saw your text message," I said.

He asked me how my day was and he wanted to know when my next doctor's appointment was. We talked on the phone for over an hour like we were in high school.

All of a sudden, Shawn got serious. "Hope the real reason I called you today was to let you know that my divorce is final." We were both silent for the next few minutes. I honestly didn't know what to say, so I was glad when he continued. "I know I told you I would give you some time and I'm not trying to pressure you, but Hope, I've missed you. Knowing you are carrying my child only makes me admire you more. I can never apologize enough for the way I handled things. I guess I'm asking you for another chance. But I want to do things your way."

I couldn't believe what I was hearing. I never thought I would have another chance with Shawn, but I wasn't ready to make a decision. I really needed to pray and ask God for direction. The conversation I had with Chloe and Tamera earlier came to mind and I realized that I didn't have to make a decision right then.

"Shawn, I don't know what to say. I just need a little time, I don't want us trying to rebuild a relationship just because I'm pregnant. Can you please be patient with me?" I asked him.

I could hear Shawn sigh on the other end of the phone and I imagined him rubbing his hand down his face.

Hope's Faith   *Raegan Dennis*

"That's fair, but I'm not giving up on us Hope," he said sounding defeated.

We ended our phone call with Shawn promising to call me the next day.

CHAPTER 14

My pregnancy was progressing much better than anyone anticipated. Every doctor's appointment Dr. Goldman told me how he was amazed by how well things were going. I owed all credit to God, I knew there was no way I would have made if God was not in this. Things had even been getting better with Shawn. He respected my wishes and gave me as much time as I needed and never pressured me to define our relationship.

I had just turned six months and I finally felt like I was out of the danger zone. Shawn and I had just left the doctor's office but I really wasn't ready for our time to end. He helped me into the passenger seat of his SUV and asked if I was hungry.

"I would absolutely love a salad with everything in it and lots of ranch dressing," I said while my mouth was watering at the thought of satisfying my craving.

"Sounds good, we can stop by Niki's real quick and I'll run in and get your salad," Shawn said while putting his seatbelt on.

Niki's had the best salad in Charlotte, the grilled chicken and real bacon on top was a meal by itself.

"Can we eat there?" I asked, I knew I was pressing my luck, but I was so tired of being in the house, this one time couldn't hurt.

He gave me the side eye before he responded. "Hope, you know what the doctor said, you still need to be off of your feet. We don't need anything putting you in jeopardy of preterm labor. I will go in grab your food and get you home, off of your feet."

I folded my arms over my chest and poked out my bottom lip going into full pout mode. I looked out the window to avoid looking at him. I knew he was right, but he didn't know what it was like to be stuck in the same four walls day after day, week after week, month after month.

"Don't be like that, please, I just want what is best for you and the baby," he said his voice full of sympathy. I turned around in my seat so I could look at him.

"You have no idea what it's like to sit in the house day in and day out. I'm not asking to go walk Northlake mall, I just want to have one meal outside of my tiny apartment, I'll be sitting down the whole time." I said hoping that was enough to convince him.

"Just this one time Hope," he said as we turned into the small Niki's small parking lot.

I was so excited that I had the opportunity to do something else besides going to the doctor and right back home. Shawn walked around to the passenger side of his SUV and opened my door. He helped me out of the car and waited while I adjusted my heather gray sweatshirt dress. I was glad that my feet weren't as swollen as they had been so I could actually fit my gray and white shell toe Adidas. Shawn was dressed down in dark blue jeans and a white Polo shirt with all white Forces on. I couldn't help but admire how handsome he looked. He grabbed my hand pulling me toward the front door of the restaurant. Niki's was extremely small but always packed. It was only open for breakfast and lunch so it stayed busy from five in the morning when it opened until two in the afternoon when it closed.

We found a booth in the corner and I sat down while Shawn went to order our food. Shawn came back to our table a few minutes later with my Niki's salad and fried chicken wings with French fries for himself. Before we started eating I reached for his hand prepared to bless the food.

However, he caught me totally off guard when he began praying over our meal. "Father, thank you for this food and thank you for our daughter, please continue to keep her and her mother safe. Amen." I just looked at him and smiled. "Surprised?" He asked me raising his eyebrow.

"Just a little, but that's a pleasant surprise." I said looking into his hazel eyes. I reached for my lemonade and took a long sip without breaking eye contact.

"What's on your mind?" He asked matching my stare.

Just as I was about to answer, I heard a familiar voice that made the hair on my arm stand up. I heard this voice only once, but there was no mistaking who it belonged to.

"Yeah, what is on your mind? I would like to know myself." The owner of the voice was now standing directly in front of the booth Shawn and I were sitting in.

She was taller than me by at least four inches. She looked like she may have been biracial by her light brown complexion. Her reddish-brown hair was naturally curly and it was piled on top of her head in a messy bun. Her makeup was on point topped off by false lashes and nude lip gloss. The black and red bodycon dress she had on made me extremely insecure the way it hugged her in all the right places. It was something how fast a woman could size up another woman in thirty seconds or less. The way she was looking, I knew I was being sized up as well.

"Alana, this is Hope, Hope, this is my ex-wife Alana." Shawn introduced us trying to keep his composure.

"So this is why you were in such a rush to divorce me?" Alana asked as she looked down at me. "I clearly recall telling you to stay away from my husband, if it were not for you, we would be happy right now. How does it feel to be a homewrecker?"

I was about to get up and give her a piece of my mind, but Shawn put his hand over mine and shook his head before he spoke. "Alana, you wrecked your own home, you left and thought you could just come back when you realized the grass wasn't greener wherever you went. You cleaned out the bank account and left me with an empty house. You did that. Hope came along and fixed what you wrecked."

"Shawn, let's go, she is not worth our time," I said while rubbing my baby bump with one hand and closing the Styrofoam container my salad was in with the other.

"You're pregnant, she's pregnant?" Alana practically screamed, knocking my salad on the floor. Now that's where she messed up, you don't mess with a pregnant woman's food. Especially something she had been craving.

"Let me tell you something" I said getting out of my seat, "It's nothing more pathetic than a woman wanting a man that does not want her, now if you will excuse me, we are done here."

I made my way out of the booth with Shawn right behind me. We left Alana standing there and I hoped she wouldn't follow us outside. I was walking or waddling as fast as I could to get to Shawn's SUV.

"Hope, baby, I'm so sorry," Shawn said as he opened the car door for me.

He helped me into the seat and looked at me for a few seconds before making his way to the driver's side. He rubbed his hand down his face letting me know he was frustrated. We were both quiet as he drove until I broke the silence.

"She's beautiful." I don't know why I allowed her presence to bother me so much. Shawn reached in my lap and took my left hand in his.

"You are beautiful, inside and out. Please don't ever compare yourself to her. I'm exactly where I want to be," he tried his best to reassure me.

I closed my eyes and allowed the tears to fall that I had been holding back since I heard Alana's voice. I wasn't sure if I could blame these tears on pregnancy hormones or fear that I wasn't enough for Shawn. I had no intentions on crying in front of him, but the tears wouldn't stop, and I didn't try to stop them.

CHAPTER 15

By the time we made it back to my apartment, I had fallen asleep. That was another unexplained pregnancy mystery, you could fall asleep virtually anywhere. Shawn parked beside my silver Honda Accord but didn't move out of his seat. He was still holding my hand when I opened my eyes. I looked around the parking lot and was relieved my mom's car was gone. Since I was in Shawn's care that day, she had made plans to visit some of her old friends.

We made our way up to my apartment and I was glad to be home. I wish I would have listened to Shawn and got our food to go, but it was too late for the should have game. I took my shoes off and Shawn put my feet in his lap. I grabbed the remote off the coffee table and handed it to him. I knew I was going to fall asleep again so I got comfortable as he rubbed my feet while channel surfing.

Just as I was getting into a deep sleep, I jumped up startled at the sound of glass breaking and a car alarm going off. I lived in a quiet apartment complex and we rarely had these types of incidents. Shawn jumped up and opened my balcony door. "Oh my God," he screamed as he got his car keys off the coffee table and hit the button to deactivate his car alarm.

He ran out of the door before I could ask him anything. I got up to and walked barefoot to my balcony, when I looked out at the parking lot I put my hand over my mouth because I was in complete disbelief. Shawn's Nissan Armada was sitting on four flat tires, the windshield was shattered and the driver side window was busted out. As if that wasn't bad enough there was red paint poured all over the hood.

A few of my neighbors had come outside to see what all the commotion was about. The complex security guard drove up and got out of his fake police car. He approached Shawn, but I couldn't make out what they were saying. They talked for a few minutes when the security guard went to his car and got a card and gave it to Shawn. A few minutes later the real police showed up. I really wanted to hear what they were saying, but I knew I had to wait until Shawn came back in. I was starting to get a headache which sometimes happened when my blood pressure was higher than it needed to be, so I decided to go lie back down on the sofa. I knew exactly who was responsible for vandalizing Shawn's SUV.

She must of followed us back to my apartment. I couldn't believe she would go through all of this trouble to get the attention of a man that made it clear that he did not want her. Now she knew where I lived, so I had to be extremely cautious. I couldn't wait to tell Chloe and Hope about everything that had taken place in just one day. Shawn finally came back in with his head down. He sat down on the sofa and put my feet back in his lap.

"I can't believe she would bring this to your house. Baby I'm sorry," he said rubbing my feet.

I couldn't help but notice that was the second time he called me baby that day. I did know this was not the appropriate time to bring it up, so I put that in the back of my mind for the moment.

"Stop apologizing for something you have no control over," I said resting my hands on my stomach.

"The good news is your complex has cameras and the security guard said he will be able to pull the tape so I'll have evidence to press charges if I choose to." He told me still giving my feet his undivided attention. "My Insurance company will cover the cost of all the damages as long as I can provide a police report, so as far as the car is concerned have nothing to worry about. But as far as you are concerned, I am worried. I don't like the fact that Alana knows where you live." He just looked at me for a minute.

"Are you okay?" he asked

I was starting to have some cramping but I didn't think it was a big deal. "I'm fine, it has just been a long event filled day," I said rubbing my stomach where it was beginning to tighten. "I think I just need some sleep."

Shawn gave me a look that let me know he wasn't sure if he believed me. His cell phone rang and he answered on the first ring telling the caller he would be right down.

"That's the tow truck bae, I'll be right back." He said and kissed me on the forehead.

Two babies and one bae in one day, I couldn't lie to myself and say I didn't like these terms of endearment, because I did, but we had a few things to iron out before I got caught up in my feelings again or was I already caught up?

One of the things the nurses at the hospital taught me was to lie on my side if I started cramping. I was hoping that if I did that it would alleviate some of the cramps I'd been having.

As I was getting in a more comfortable position I realized I was actually alone, so I decided to use that rare opportunity to pray. "Lord, I know you wouldn't bring me and my baby this far to leave us. Please keep her safe and let her bake a little longer. Order my steps where Shawn is concerned, help me to do what is pleasing in your sight. In the name of Jesus amen. No sooner than that amen left my lips, the voice of God spoke to me, but I wasn't sure if I heard correctly the first time. I didn't have to second guess because the next time I heard it loud and clear.

"Pray for her, pray for Alana."

CHAPTER 16

I had added Alana to my daily prayer list. The first few days were extremely hard. I was still mad that she knocked over my Niki's salad and ruined the only chance I had to be somewhere other than home or the doctor's office. The first few prayers were something like God please bless Alana. Then I would get convicted and have to ask for forgiveness. Gradually my prayers for her became more sincere and heartfelt. One day it hit me like a ton of bricks, the more I prayed for Alana, the better I felt, the more at peace I was.

Of course the tape the security guard pulled showed Alana slicing all four of Shawn's tires, pouring a can of red paint on the hood and throwing two bricks, one on the windshield the other in the driver's side window. All while wearing that same red and black dress and red stilettos. It took quite a few weeks for all of the damage to be repaired on his car and he had just dropped off the rental car he was driving and picked up his Armada. Shawn absolutely wanted to press charges but I wasn't sure if that was the right thing to do. He could easily go to court and tell the judge he didn't want to press charges. He already had a restraining order against her which I did agree with. The court date was coming up and I could tell Shawn was a little nervous. He had come by my apartment after work which had become a daily routine for us. I was in my usual spot on the sofa with my feet in his lap.

"What do you think will happen at court next week?" I asked enjoying my daily foot rub.

"When I talked to the district attorney, he said if I press charges Alana will have to reimburse me for the deductible I paid to get my car fixed and she will probably just get community service since this is her first offense," he told me.

I sat up a little so I could gage his reaction to what I was about to say. "I've been praying for her, I really didn't want to at first but the holy spirit led me to pray for her. I can't explain it, but the more I pray for her, the more at peace I feel."

Shawn moved my feet out of his lap and got up. I didn't know what to expect, but I know I wasn't expecting what happened. He kneeled in front of me as I sat all the way up. He took both of my hands in his and what he said next blew me away.

"That's why I love you, I love you Hope."

I looked into those hazel eyes trying to see straight through him. Of course I started crying, I didn't think I would have any tears left by the time I delivered. He took one of his hands and wiped my tears with his thumb. "I hope these are happy tears." He said as he continued to wipe away my tears.

I leaned forward so my head was resting on his chest. We stayed like that until we heard the front door open. I pulled back and wiped my face. Shawn got up and shook my dad's hand and kissed my mom on the cheek.

My dad, always the more considerate parent spoke first. "We didn't mean to interrupt you young people."

My mother obviously didn't feel the same way my as my dad. "It looks like we interrupted just in time, this is why we are in this situation now." My mom voiced her opinion as she made her way to the kitchen to help my dad put away the groceries they bought.

I loved my parents dearly but I would be glad when they went back to St. George. The longer my mother stayed, the more of the mother of my childhood came out.

"Val, leave them alone. I'm excited about the situation as you call it, I'm ready to be a paw-paw," my dad defended me.

"Of course I'm happy about my granddaughter, but if we waited this long, we could have waited until she got married," my mom said as if I wasn't present for the conversation.

"Okay mom, we all know how you feel, but can you respect the fact that I have company," I said trying not to show how upset I really.

"Company, who is company? Hope you have this man in your apartment every day. Do you think God is pleased with your behavior? And what about your neighbors, I can't imagine what they must be thinking," my mom was on a roll now.

At least I knew what this was really about. This was cosmetology school all over again. If it didn't fit into Valerie Daniel's plans, it wasn't right.

"Mom, I could care less what my neighbors think, they don't have a heaven or hell to put me in. You are always trying to use God, when it's really you, you want me to please. You were embarrassed that I didn't go to four year college telling your friends I was just taking a year off to find myself. Criticizing every decision I made that didn't fit in your plan. God has forgiven me, are you going to?" I didn't mean to raise my voice but I was so angry I couldn't think straight. But I wasn't finished yet. "Where is the loving comforting mother that was here when we thought we might lose this baby? Or is this like when I was a little girl and I only got the caring mom when I was sick? And one more thing, you begged me to tell Shawn, now that he is apart of my life it's a problem. You never want what I want for me mom, this is my life, not yours."

My stomach was cramping and my baby girl was balling up at the bottom of my stomach. I was trying my best to calm down but I could not stop crying. I was rubbing my stomach trying to get the baby to move hoping that would ease up the pain. My dad came over to the sofa after giving my mother a look I had never seen from him before.

"Shawn, help me get Hope in the bed, she needs to rest," my dad said putting one of his arms through one of mine. Shawn mimicked my dad's movement and they gently lifted me off of the sofa. And that's when it happened, my water broke.

CHAPTER 17

To say I was scared would have been an understatement. I was only a little over seven months pregnant. Everything had been going so well I just assumed I would make it closer to my due date. I wasn't due until December and it was only the end of September. My dad and Shawn helped me down the one flight of stairs that led to the parking lot. Shawn's car was closer so that's where I was led. My dad and Shawn had a brief discussion and they decided to let Shawn get me to the hospital and my parents would meet us there shortly.

I closed my eyes as I was silently prayed, for my baby to be okay, I wouldn't be able to handle it if something went wrong. Shawn reached over and grabbed my hand while he drove with the other trying to get me to the hospital as fast as he could. I rubbed my stomach with my free hand but nothing was easing the pain that seemed to get increasingly worse.

I was immediately taken up to labor and delivery when we arrived at the hospital. I had changed into the hospital gown and was sitting up in the bed waiting for the nurse to come back.

"Can you call Chloe and Tamera?" I asked Shawn when the latest pain eased up.

I reached for my phone that I had laid on the bedside table so I could hand it to him. I closed my eyes as another round of pain began. The nurse, who had introduced herself as Kenya, came back to check my cervix, take my vitals and hook me up to the baby monitor to see if I was in false labor or if this was the real thing. The way I felt, this was definitely the real thing. My blood pressure was elevated and the contractions were about eight minutes apart. I was definitely in labor.

"We have talked to Dr. Goldman and he is on the way. He is going to have to remove your cerclage since your bag of water has ruptured," Kenya told me as she looked at the paper coming out of the machine that measured my contractions and the baby's heartbeat.

I couldn't believe I went from listening to Shawn tell me he loved me, to arguing with my mother, to being in labor in a matter of minutes. Shawn stood beside the bed and held my hand.

"Chloe and Tamera should be here soon," he informed me.

I was grateful my best friends were willing to drop whatever they were doing to be apart of my support system.

Once Dr. Goldman arrived things moved quickly. The contractions were causing the baby's heart rate to drop significantly and my blood pressure was steadily increasing. Dr. Goldman told me the best thing to do was to have a C-section.

"At thirty weeks, the baby should be fine once we deliver, but she will be in the NICU for a while so her lungs can have time to mature, but it will better to get her out as soon as we can, for yours and her safety," my doctor said looking at the same paper the nurse had just been looking at. "Nurse, let's get Hope prepped for surgery," he said while walking out of the room.

Tamera came in my room followed by Chloe. Shawn informed them of everything that happened as he stepped back and allowed my friends to be by my side.

"Where are your mom and dad? " Chloe asked me looking around the room. Shawn and I exchanged looks before he answered for me.

"They should be here any minute, we drove separate cars." I was so glad that Shawn stepped in with an answer because I wasn't prepared to tell my friends what happened between me and my mom. The door to my room opened again and this time it was my parents.

My dad came over to my bed leaned down and kissed me on the forehead and whispered in my ear. "I'm sorry baby girl." I appreciated my dad's apology but I really felt like it should have come from my mother.

"So what is the doctor saying? " My dad asked Shawn.

Before he could answer someone came to take me to the operating room. My nurse Kenya came in to ask who would go in the operating room with me.

"Operating room?" My mom finally spoke, but it wasn't to me. Shawn spoke up to answer the nurse and my mom at the same time.

"I'll be going with Hope for the C-section."

Kenya looked around the room as she informed my family of what to expect. "Everyone else is more than welcome to stay here in Hope's room, we will keep you posted with her and the baby's progress." I was then wheeled out with Shawn beside me holding my hand.

I wasn't able to hold my baby right away since she was premature. I didn't care what the doctors said, she was perfect to in my eyes. Being born at only three pounds and eight ounces, my baby girl would have to spend some time in the NICU so her lungs could continue to develop and she gain some weight. One of the nurses from NICU came to let Shawn and me know that we would be able to spend some time with our baby girl once I was out of recovery.

I woke up to see Shawn looking at me with a smile on his face. We were still in the recovery area so it was just us two and a nurse who came to check on me periodically. I was glad to have some alone time with him after everything that had happened that day.

"You are beautiful" he said and I just smiled back at him.

I never wanted this feeling to end and I could only hope he felt the same way. Our short lived private moment was interrupted by the nurse letting us know someone would be taking me back to my room. If it was up to me, I would have stayed where I was but I knew my parents and best friends were waiting on me.

CHAPTER 18

Leaving my baby girl in the hospital was the hardest thing I ever had to do. Shawn and I were in our new favorite place, the NICU, spending time with our daughter before he took me home. She looked so tiny in her incubator with all the tubes she was hooked up to help her breath.

"You know we have to name her before we leave," I said looking at Shawn, then back at the baby.

"Do you have anything in mind bae?" He asked me looking at our perfect creation.

"I haven't really thought about it, I was so focused on trying to stay pregnant, I didn't really think about after she was born. But I know if it wasn't for God, we wouldn't have made it this far," I said not taking my eyes off of her.

"I really do admire your faith in God, I can only hope one day my faith is as strong as yours," Shawn said looking at me with those mesmerizing eyes of his.

That's when I knew what my baby's name was. "That's it. Faith, I think we should name her Faith," I said as I reached over to hug him.

"I love it," he said smiling as I pulled back from our hug.

I wasn't ready to leave Faith Danielle King, but the nurses assured me they would take good care of her. Since Shawn and I were her parents we could come visit pretty much anytime we wanted to. Shawn called the high school to take some of his vacation days so he could go with me to the hospital for my daily visits. I never dreamed we would be getting along so well after the breakup, the discovery of his ex-wife, and me keeping the pregnancy from him. That just proved that God could turn any situation around and make it work for your good. If God could do all of those things, I had to believe the relationship I had with my mom could be mended.

It felt great to go home and know I could stay there without someone being with me at all times. My dad told me he thought it would be best if he and my mom stayed at a hotel until it was time for them to go back to St. George. I hated for my dad to feel like they weren't welcome in my home, but I knew what my dad said was best. I also knew I had to get my spare bedroom transformed a nursery for when I was able to bring Faith home.

The first thing I planned to do was to take an uninterrupted nap. I was exhausted from the past few months and I needed to get as much rest as possible before Faith came home. When Shawn and I walked into my apartment, I was shocked to see my parents, my two best friends, Cassandra, and even Ms. Claire, and a few of my clients in my living room.

"Welcome home," everybody screamed in unison.

There were pink and white balloons everywhere. I looked to my right to see my dining room table covered with all types of food. There was fried chicken, barbecue meatballs, macaroni and cheese, and fruit trays, and that wasn't even everything. In the middle of the table there was a white sheet cake that was decorated with pink icing.

"When did you guys plan all of this?" I asked walking around to give everyone a hug.

Surprisingly, my mom was the one who answered. "Well, we never had a baby shower, and we know you needed virtually everything, so we decided to surprise you." I knew that was my mom's way of saying she was sorry. She would never verbalize an apology, so I took what I could get. I walked over to where my mom was standing and gave her a hug. She looked at me holding both of my hands in hers. "You are going to make a great mother pumpkin, better than I've ever been," she said and hugged me one more time.

We all sat down to eat and everybody had questions about the labor and delivery. That led to an open discussion about labor. Each woman that had children shared their labor story and no two were the same. Some were funny, some were unbelievable, some were even sad. But hearing one of my clients tell us about her son that was born at twenty seven weeks and is now a healthy athletic ten year old gave me confidence that Faith would be just fine.

Shawn helped me open all the gifts which ranged from simple things like diapers and wipes to more extravagant gifts like a stroller and a baby swing.

"I can't thank y'all enough," I said with tears streaming down my face. I didn't know how long it would take for those hormones to get back to normal, but I would be glad when it happened.

"That's not all" Chloe said getting up from the sofa. I couldn't imagine anything else, this was already more than enough.

Chloe grabbed my hand and led me to my spare bedroom. There were pink wooden letters on the door that spelled out FAITH. I couldn't help but wonder how they got my daughter's name on the door, considering we had just named her that day. As if reading my thoughts, Tamera gave an explanation.

"Shawn sent your dad a text message once y'all came up with a name and I ran to Michael's to get the letters."

I couldn't believe they pulled this off in such a short period of time.

"Speaking of Shawn, where did he go?" I asked looking down the hall. No one answered me, but I really wanted him to see what my friends and family had done for us. As I tried to move back to go down the hall to look for him, Tamera stopped me.

"Just open the door Hope, you may find just what you are looking for," she said with a smile.

I opened the door to what was once an extra bedroom to see a fully decorated, furnished nursery. There was a cherry wood crib with pink and white bedding. There was also a matching changing table, dresser and gliding rocking chair. I was in awe at what I was seeing, but there were no words to describe what I saw next, Shawn on one knee holding an open black velvet box that held a one carat solitaire diamond ring set in white gold. I walked over to where he was as he stood up.

"Hope, will you marry me?" He asked me his hazel eyes never leaving mine.

I put my hand over my mouth and nodded my head, unable to speak. He placed the ring on my left ring finger and it fit perfectly.

"Well I guess that's a yes" my dad said coming over to shake Shawn's hand.

"It's definitely a yes," I said while holding up my hand to admire my engagement ring.

I was exhausted but there was no way I could sleep after the day I had just experienced. Everyone had left my apartment and Shawn and I were sitting on the sofa watching a movie. My head was resting on his chest, I was more into listening to his heartbeat than the movie we were watching. This was the first time since I went into labor that we had any alone time. I was enjoying our time together and I couldn't wait until this was our permanent life.

"It's getting late, I better get home," Shawn said sitting up.

I knew he was right but that didn't make me stop from not wanting him to leave. I got up so I could walk him to the door. He reached out to hug me as we stood in front of the door.

"Shawn, I need you to ask you something, but I need you to be completely honest," I said pulling back so I could look at him.

"Should I be scared?" He asked me walking me back to the sofa so we could sit down.

"No, I just want us to start out the right way," I said turning to face him. "You are okay with us not having sex until after the wedding right?" I was a little afraid to hear his answer. I know he said the real reason we broke up had nothing to do with sex, but in my mind it was still a determining factor for him.

He grabbed my hands before he answered. "I would never ask you to compromise your faith for me again. I already knew we would be waiting before I even proposed to you. I want you for a lifetime, and whatever I have to do to get you for a lifetime, I'll do it." At that moment I knew everything I had just been through was worth it.

"If you are willing to do anything, does that include premarital counseling? My pastor, Pastor Wright, won't marry us if we don't do the counseling, plus I think it will be good for us." I don't know why I was so nervous to hear his answer, he had proven to be an even better man than I remembered.

"I think that's a great idea, just set it up, tell me the time and place and I'm there" he said. "I was going to talk to you about this later, but there is no time like the present, so there is no point in waiting."

When he said that I immediately got nervous. I started imagining the worst possible thing he could tell me. Was it about Alana? Was there another child out there I knew nothing about? I was so busy with my imagination that I had to ask him to repeat himself.

"You are that surprised, you have to hear it again" he said smiling. I was going to let him think that, I didn't want him to think I wasn't listening to him.

"You heard me right, I want what you have with God. Just watching you the last few months helped me see that anything is possible with God. You have peace in your life even with things being crazy as they have been. And seeing our daughter survive after all you have been through, that is a miracle."

I hugged Shawn with tears streaming down my face. To hear Shawn say he wanted a relationship with God made me realize that anything really was possible. The Lord never ceased to amaze me. We both got up from the sofa and walked toward the door. Shawn hugged me one last time and placed a soft peck on my lips. I looked into his hazel eyes and got to say what I had been waiting almost a week to say. "I love you too."

CHAPTER 19

Shawn decided not to press charges against Alana for what she did to his car. I was glad he decided not because I felt like that would have brought on more drama. He still had the restraining order against her, so we hadn't had any more problems from her. We did decide to start looking for a place to live once we were married, neither of us were comfortable knowing she knew where I lived. Shawn still lived in the house he once shared with Alana and my apartment wasn't big enough for me, him, Faith, and the things we wanted to keep from each of our homes.

I was on my laptop at the dining room table looking at houses online. I was waiting on Shawn so we could go to the hospital to see Faith when there was a knock at my door. I just assumed it was Shawn, so I opened the door without looking through the peephole. I opened the door smiling, but that vanished when I saw who was standing in my doorway.

"Can I come in?" Alana asked me.

I was glad she was much calmer than she was the last time I saw her. I stepped back so she could come in and gestured for her to have a seat at the dining room table.

I sat down across from her and waited for her to tell me why she was there. "I wanted to do this sooner, but Shawn is always here, and I'm sure you know about the restraining order."

My curiosity got the best of me so I had to ask. "How would you know how much Shawn is here?"

She looked down as if she was ashamed. "I've been wanting to talk to you, but every time I came by I saw Shawn's car so I never stopped." I couldn't imagine what she had to talk to me about and I prayed things wouldn't get ugly.

"I wanted to apologize to you, the way I acted at Niki's, what I did to Shawn's car in your parking lot, none of that was called for. I was just so angry," she said looking at me. "You see, Shawn had never rejected me, I know I didn't treat him well, but no matter what I did, he was always forgave me. So I figured that time would be no different. I got caught up with the worst type of man. He was so different from Shawn. I thought that was a good thing. He convinced me to move to Atlanta with him. He said he ran his own businesses and he could invest money for me and I'd get a huge profit. So I cleaned out the joint bank account Shawn and I had and sold everything we owned. Things slowly went from dream come true to nightmare. I was being showered with gifts and trips constantly, but eventually that stopped. I would ask him about the money I gave him to invest and he would tell me not to worry that I would begin seeing money soon. I mean I gave him over ten thousand dollars, all the money Shawn and I had saved for a down payment on a house. One day it was like a switch went off. I asked about the money again and he flipped out. He beat me like I was a man in the street. That went on for a while until I was able to get away from him. I came back thinking Shawn would be glad to have me back, but you were already in his life." Alana was in tears by the time she finished telling me her story.

"Alana, I'm so sorry you had to go through that," I said getting up to get her some tissue.

I handed Alana the tissue and she grabbed my hand to look at my engagement ring. There was a moment of silence as she studied my ring.

"Congratulations, Shawn deserves some happiness and I think he found it with you." Alana sounded so defeated at that moment. "I just wanted to apologize, I didn't mean to dump all of that on you." She stood up and started walking toward the door.

"Alana," I said causing her to turn around and face me. "Thank you, your apology means a lot to me." I reached out to give her a hug, and she actually hugged me back. I silently asked God to heal her heart as we said our goodbyes.

When the holy spirit led me to pray for Alana, never would I have imagined her apologizing to me. I knew that I would continue to pray for her, I could tell she had some issues that she needed to work out, but all I could do was keep praying. I tried to get back on my laptop and continue my search for houses, but I'd lost my focus. I was still amazed by what God was doing all around me. I closed my laptop and moved from the dining room table to the sofa. I had to take a moment to thank God for all he had done. I carried my baby girl longer than expected, I was about to marry her father, who had completely surrendered his life to God and my mom and I were working on our relationship.

Someone knocking on the door brought me out of my personal time with the Lord. I got up and walked to the door. Not prepared for anymore surprises, I looked out the peephole this time. I opened the door to let my future husband in. I stood on my toes, put my arms around his neck and kissed him on the lips.

"You ready to go see the princess," he asked.

"I'm always ready to see my baby girl, but sit down first, we need to talk," I said heading to the sofa. "I had some unexpected company today." I reached over and grabbed his hand.

"Who?" He asked looking confused.

"Alana came by, before you get upset, let me tell you why," I said hoping he wouldn't get upset. I relayed what happened when Alana came by. I even told him what he told me about her abusive ex.

Shawn waited a few minutes before he said anything. "She didn't try anything did she?"

I just looked at him and shook my head. "Baby it wasn't even like that, she seemed sad, almost defeated. But she did say she thinks you found happiness with me."

He seemed to relax when I said that. "She's right about that, you make me very happy and I can't wait to spend the rest of my life with you. Now we have a princess to go see."

CHAPTER 20

My parents were back in St. George and I did miss them, but I think the distance was good for me and my mom while we were working on our relationship. She had been trying to convince my dad to move back to Charlotte so they could be close to Faith and help raise her. I didn't even have to object because my dad had no intentions of uprooting their life.

They put a lot of time and money into renovating my grandmother's house and my dad had to remind my mom of that. My dad had put the discussion to rest several times, but my mom found a way to bring it up every time we talked. I don't know why I thought this time would be different.

"Mom, you know dad is not going to sell the house or rent it out to somebody who is not going to appreciate all the work y'all put into it. Not to mention y'all would have to find something to rent here." I was trying my best to reason with her, but she wasn't making it easy.

"We can always stay with you and Shawn," she said like it was the most logical thing to do.

"Val, leave that girl alone, nobody is moving back to Charlotte." I heard my dad yelling at my mom in the background. "The kids need a chance to start their life without two old people in their business."

I chuckled to myself making sure my mom didn't hear me. "Put your phone on speaker," I told my mom so my dad could hear as well. "Shawn's dad and younger brother will be here in a few weeks and we want you to come up so you can meet them." I was excited to meet Shawn's family, I just hoped my mom behaved herself.

"What about his mother, she isn't coming?" My mom asked. It was an innocent question, but I was grateful she asked me and not Shawn.

"He lost his mother at a young age," I informed her. "She died in a car accident leaving his dad alone to raise him and his younger brother. So can you guys make sure you make them feel a part of the family?"

I really wanted everyone to get along. Being an only child I always wanted a big family and it seemed like my wish was slowly coming true. As soon as I got off the phone with my parents it rang again. I looked at the caller ID and knew this was not a friendly call.

"Hello," I said waiting on Tamera to say something about our lack of communication lately.

"Well, hello is all you have to say to one of your best friends that you haven't had a conversation with in God knows when."

I knew she was going to be upset, maybe if I explained how busy I had been she would understand. "Between going back and forth to the hospital to see Faith, premarital counseling sessions and looking for a house, I haven't had any time for myself." Did I just hear her suck her teeth?
"I'm sure I know who you do have time for these days," she said with a hint of sarcasm.

"We do have a lot to catch up on", I said, "so let's make plans to get together soon. Do you know what Chloe's schedule is like? Maybe we can do dinner one day next week."

I didn't want to be one of those women who got a man and put her friends on the back burner. I was thankful that Tamera called me out before I was too far gone.

"You should call Chloe and see what days she is available," Tamera suggested putting emphasis on the word you.

"Okay, I'll call her as soon as we get off the phone," I agreed. We talked a little while longer before I hung up with her and I called Chloe.

Chloe didn't answer so I left her a voicemail to call me back as soon as she could. No soon as I put the phone down Chloe was calling me right back.

"Hey stranger," she said, "to what do I owe this phone call?" Had I been that bad of a friend?

"What's your schedule like next week?" I asked hoping she would see I was making an effort to spend time with her and Tamera. "Maybe we can do dinner, and since I'm not pregnant anymore we can go get sushi."

My phone beeped indicating I had another call coming in, I pulled the phone away from my face and saw Shawn's hazel eyes and smiling face on my screen. I decided not to answer and give Chloe my undivided attention, I would just call him back when I was finished talking to her.

"I'm open, the Lord hasn't blessed me with a boo yet, so I'm available whenever you can squeeze little old me in," she said laughing.

"Monday we have an appointment to look at a house, Tuesdays and Thursdays are our premarital counseling sessions, and Wednesday we always stay at the hospital late." Just saying that out loud made me realize I was going to have to find a way to balance everything.

Once Faith came home, and I went back to the salon my time would be even more limited than it was now. I didn't even want to think about planning a wedding and being a wife.

"Chloe, do you think I'm ready for all of this? I haven't really experienced being a mom yet with Faith still in the hospital, so I'll be learning to be a mom and a wife virtually at the same time," I thought out loud. As always Chloe's logical thinking helped ease some of the anxiety I was feeling.

"Of course the transition is not going to be easy, but you have Shawn, you have Tamera and me. You know your mom will drop everything if you needed her help for a while. Just think about it, most of the things consuming your time now are temporary. Faith will be home soon, so you won't be going to the hospital every day, the counseling sessions will end in a few weeks, and you will find a house so that eliminates all the open houses and viewings." Chloe said easing my mind with each word she said.

Chloe was right, everything that we were doing was temporary and I couldn't allow those things to overtake me. Chloe was at work, so we couldn't talk long. We were able to finalize our dinner plans for the following Friday. We ended our phone call with me promising to call both of my best friends more often.

I still needed to return Shawn's phone call, before he called me back. Since he had returned to work, he still made sure we communicated several times a day. During our counseling sessions with Pastor Wright, we were able to figure out that the breakdown of our relationship in the beginning was communication. She told us every session that as long as kept open communication with God and each other, we would have a successful marriage. I was a little apprehensive to tell my pastor about my engagement and who I was engaged to because of the way things ended.

But a true woman of God always forgives and she did just that once she heard the whole story. I really think she was more upset with me for keeping the pregnancy hidden from Shawn for as long as I did.

I called Shawn's phone only to be sent to voicemail, when I looked at the time I figured he was on his lunch when he called but was probably back in the classroom. I was going to leave a message but I got a text message alert. I opened my text messages to see I had a new message from Shawn.

Back in class... Just wanted to hear your voice. See you tonight. Love you.

I quickly replied to his message.

Can't wait to see you! Love you too!

With nothing else to do, I decided to take a trip to the hospital to see my baby girl. I only had a few more weeks of maternity leave left and I wanted to spend as much time with her as I could before I went back to work. Grabbing my purse and my keys, I headed out grateful for what God was doing in my life.

CHAPTER 21

I was getting dressed for my dinner with Tamera and Chloe when Shawn walked into my bedroom. I was looking in the full length mirror trying to decide if the third outfit I had tried on was the one.

"Wow, you are absolutely the most beautiful woman I have ever laid eyes on," he complimented me.

I looked down so he couldn't see me blushing. "Thank you, you are pretty handsome yourself," I said still looking down.

"How would you know, you aren't even looking at me," he laughed while tilting my chin up so I could look at him.

"So what do you think?" I asked him referring to the black knee length sweater dress and black leather knee boots.

"I think you better get out of here before we have to find somebody to marry us tonight," he said before kissing me on the lips allowing this kiss to linger a little longer than normal.

I was feeling a little unsure about wearing something fitted because I hadn't lost all of my baby weight yet, but the way Shawn was responding to me, I had nothing to be unsure about. I pulled away from our kiss before things got out of control and grabbed my black leather moto jacket off the bed. We walked out of my room each of us in search of our car keys. Shawn walked me out and to my car for one last kiss.

"Call me when you get home," he said walking toward his SUV. I gave him one last look as I got in my car thanking God for my husband to be.

I met my girls at Kabuto, a Japanese steak house, on W.T. Harris boulevard. I saw that Chloe was already in the waiting area. I walked over and gave her a hug.

"Don't you look cute?" I said admiring her fitted jeans, red blazer and red stilettos. She was even wearing her hair flat ironed which reached past her shoulders.

"Thank you sis, but I must say, for someone who just had a baby, I'm impressed,," she said looking me up and down.

"Where is Tamera?" I asked. I was ten minutes late myself so I assumed I would be the last to arrive.

"Some things will never change, you know she is late for everything," Chloe said looking at her phone. "She sent me a text fifteen minutes ago saying she was five minutes away." We both laughed because that was Tamera code meaning she had just left the house.

Twenty minutes later all three of us were sitting in front of the hibachi talking and laughing. We opted for a private room so we could talk openly. The tables in the main dining room seated up to ten people, so if you were dining with a small party, other people were usually seated with you. I had so much to tell them, but I didn't know where to start.

"First, let me apologize to you two," I said as a waitress came to our table to take our drink orders. We all ordered sweet tea and added spider and California rolls as an appetizer. "Like I was saying, I have not been acting like a best friend to either of you lately and I need to apologize. I hope y'all can forgive me," I continued after the waitress left our table.

"Of course, we forgive you," Chloe said.

"Speak for yourself," Tamera said looking at me.

"Don't be like that, that's why I'm here." I said hoping they could hear the sincerity in my voice.

"We know your life has completely changed in the last few month and you are just adjusting to those changes," Chloe said doing her best to make me feel better.

The waitress came back to bring our drinks and appetizers. We put our orders in and waited on our chef to come to our table to start cooking our meals. I loved hibachi restaurants because the chefs were always entertaining as they cooked their food right in front of you and made jokes at the same time, and the food was amazing.

With our meals in front of us and our private room finally being private, it was time to tell my best friends what had been happening in my life. They were both shocked when I told them about Alana's visit.

"Do you think she was for real?" Tamera asked "Maybe she is trying to put your guard down," she said taking a sip of her tea.

I thought about it for a minute before I said anything. "She just seemed so defeated, I can't explain it, but I do think she was being sincere. I've been praying for her since the day she did what she did to Shawn's car. Lord knows I didn't want to, but I had to be obedient to the holy spirit. Maybe God really is working on her, she really has been through a lot."

Tamera looked at me and rolled her eyes. "Oh, that's your new best friend now?" She said and I couldn't tell if she was serious or not until she started laughing. "I applaud you for that Hope, I don't know if I would be able to do what you are doing. I would have been asking God if he was sure he was talking to me."

Chloe just shook her head at Tamera before she spoke "I think that's awesome Hope, you never know how God will bless you just for you being obedient."

We laughed and talked for hours until we practically got kicked out of the restaurant because they were about to close. We walked out of the restaurant into the cool night air and gave each other hugs.

Something that Pastor Wright said at one of our counseling sessions came to mind. People make time for what they want to make time for. These were my best friends and had been for years, and I wouldn't allow our friendship to be compromised anymore. We made plans to get together again soon and they promised to come over when Shawn's dad and brother came to town.

I couldn't remember the last time I had been out this late. Even though I was tired, I felt refreshed. I needed that time with my girls. We all balanced each other out and I always felt like I could take on anything after talking to them. I pulled into the parking lot of my apartment complex and went up the one flight of stairs. I couldn't wait to take my boots off, they were cute, but uncomfortable. When I made it into my apartment I took my boots off and removed my jacket. That's when I realized I hadn't checked my phone the whole night. I pulled my phone out of my purse and saw I had no missed calls and only one text message from Shawn.

Counting down the days until I can wake up every day to your beautiful face. Love you!

I read that message over and over until I fell asleep on the sofa with my phone in my hand.

CHAPTER 22

Shawn and I were at the hospital spending time with Faith. She was progressing better than we ever expected. She was eating on a regular schedule and picking up weight. The doctors wanted to make sure she would be able to breath on her own, that was the determining factor for when we could take her home.

"We really need to start thinking about setting a date for the wedding," Shawn said while holding Faith on his chest.

As ready as I was to become Mrs. Hope King, I didn't want to start planning until my baby was home. "I really don't want to think about dates until our little princess can be a part of the wedding," I told Shawn standing up so I could take Faith from him. I was glad she was awake so I could stare into her hazel eyes. She was the spitting image of me with her father's eyes.

"I can understand that, I'm just ready to make you my wife," Shawn said leaning back in his chair.

"Can you believe we are even sitting here with our daughter, talking about setting a wedding date? If somebody told me this was going to happen, I never would have believed them," I said not able to take my eyes off of my baby girl.

Shawn reached over and grabbed my free hand and kissed it. "I would have believed it, I knew you were the one the first time I laid eyes on you. Our moment was interrupted when one of the nurses came to Faith's area of the NICU.

"How are the parents today?" She asked taking Faith from me so she could check her vitals.

"We are good, but we would be better if we could take our princess home," Shawn answered for both of us.

The nurse gave us a smile as she spoke. "Actually Dr. Harris does want to speak to you about the possibility of discharging this angel. He is making his rounds now, so he should be here soon to talk to you." She gently handed Faith back to me before moving on to the next baby.

Just the thought of bringing Faith home seemed so unrealistic until the nurse came to talk to us. Being able to hold her anytime I wanted was something I had been praying for since the day she was born. Each day got harder and harder to leave the hospital without her.

It seemed like we had been waiting forever for the doctor to come and talk to us, but when I looked at the time it had only been forty five minutes.

"How long do you think it's going to take for the doctor to get here?" I asked trying not to show my impatience.

"He should be here any minute, I'm ready to hear what he has to say myself." Shawn leaned back his chair and closed his eyes.

I looked down at Faith and saw that she was sleeping, but I wasn't ready to put her down so I laid her on my chest and continued to wait on Dr. Harris. I looked down at my baby girl and over at my husband to be, who were both sound asleep, and silently thanked God for my family.

I had given up hope that we would talk to Dr. Harris that day. It had been two hours since the nurse came by. I heard Shawn moving around in his chair and Faith was starting to get fussy. I thought it was cute how they fell asleep and woke up at the same time. I got up to get one of the pre-made bottles of formula so I could feed my baby.

"Let me feed her," Shawn said getting up to take Faith from me. "You get a lot more time with the princess than I do," he said placing the bottle in her mouth.

"I know, it's going to be hard when I go back to work. It's so many things to figure out." I was starting to get in panic mode. I was just excited at the thought of bringing Faith home, but that quickly I allowed a tiny piece of doubt take root in my mind.

Shawn looked up at me while feeding our baby. "Tell me what we need to figure out? Remember what Pastor Wright said about communication."

I started thinking about those late nights at the salon and knew I was going to have to make major adjustments to my schedule. That led me to think about the money I may miss out on since I would no longer be available for later appointments.

"I've never had a set schedule, as a hairstylist, I've just worked according to my client's schedules. Some days would be in the salon until ten o'clock at night. Then there are the women who like the early morning six o'clock appointments. I know I won't be able to keep that up and take care of Faith. What if I start losing clients? That means I'm losing money and I need to be able to help support Faith financially."

"Slow down baby, you are making this bigger than it really is," Shawn said trying to reassure me. "We can always have your mother move back here," he said laughing.

But I didn't find that funny at all and the look on my face must have showed that I was not amused. "I'm sorry baby, I was trying to make you laugh, but I see that didn't work. Listen, we are in this together, you are not doing this alone. I'm usually leaving the school by four o'clock, so I'll be available to pick up Faith from daycare. Of course you will have to make some adjustments, all new parents do. But we are making these adjustments together. "I knew what Shawn was saying was true. I was so happy to have someone that could balance me out when the scales started tipping.

Dr. Harris finally made it to talk to us about discharging Faith from the hospital. We were already familiar with him since he was the lead doctor assigned to her care. Shawn placed a sleeping Faith in her crib and gave the doctor his attention.

Dr. Harris shook both of our hands before he told us what we had been waiting to hear. "All of us that have been on Faith's care team are very impressed with her progress. Her appetite has picked up tremendously, which means she's gaining weight. She has responded well to the antibiotics we were using to prevent any infection. The last thing on the list is her lung function. I do believe her lungs have matured enough to see how she does breathing on her own. If she proves to be able to breathe on her own, it's very possible I can discharge her as soon as next week."

Shawn and I looked at each other in disbelief. That was honestly the best thing I could have heard. Of course tears of joy made their way down my face, I was not even going to try to blame hormones, I was going to be taking my baby home and I could not have been happier. Shawn must have been feeling the same way. He hugged me and lifted me off my feet.

"Our baby is coming home," he said as he put me back down. He reached out to shake Dr. Harris's hand again. "Thank you Dr. Harris, for all you have done for our daughter." Dr. Harris returned Shawn's handshake.

"I can't take any credit, I'm only doing what God called me to do. I can certainly tell someone has been keeping your baby covered in prayer," Dr. Harris said before walking out.

My future husband looked at me and smiled. "Looks like you have a wedding to plan."

CHAPTER 23

I agreed to let my mother come and help me with Faith for the first few weeks that she was home. My parents were elated when I called to tell them Faith was being released from the hospital. My mother thought it would be a great idea for her to come help me get adjusted. In my mind, it was just a ploy for her to come and try to control my parenting. It took both Shawn and my dad to convince me that I would need the help. I did give them fair warning that if my mom tried to dictate how I mothered my daughter she would have to leave.

Things were going better than I expected with my mom. Babies definitely had a way of bringing people together. I was actually happy that my mom was here. Between planning the wedding, getting ready to move, and returning to work, I knew Shawn and I needed help with Faith. It did make me feel better that we didn't have to put her in daycare right away. It was one thing to leave her with her grandmother, but I knew I wasn't ready to leave her with a total stranger.

I was getting ready for my first day back at the salon. I had a full book and was ready to get my hands back in some hair. I still had some baby weight to lose, but considering Faith was only ten weeks old, I thought I looked pretty good. I decided to wear one of the few pairs of blue jeans I could fit with a black V-neck sweater and my black flat knee boots. I finished off my look with sterling silver hoops and a sterling silver toggle necklace. My hair had grown completely out of my pixie cut and I wasn't sure if I wanted to cut it again or let it grow so I let Tamera give me a sew-in with sixteen inch haircut in layers with a side bang.

I walked out of my bedroom and down my short hall to the living room to find my mom rocking Faith to sleep.

"Look at you, you look beautiful pumpkin," my mom complimented me. Before I could even get a thank you out of my mouth, she turned her compliment upside down. "I didn't know if I was going to like so much hair on you, but it's growing on me."

I took a deep breath before I said something I would later regret. I leaned over and kissed Faith on the forehead.

"Thanks again mom for coming up to help with the baby, Shawn and I really appreciate this," I said as I grabbed my purse and keys off of the coffee table.

I parked my Honda Accord in front of the salon, grabbed my purse and cellphone and made my way up the short walkway that led to the front door of the salon. Studio Seven was located in the historical Noda area of Charlotte. It was referred to as Noda because the area consisted of North Davidson street and surrounding streets that housed bookstores, spoken word clubs, boutiques, and all types of restaurants. The salon was a house that had been converted to a salon. I was so excited to see my clients. After doing someone's hair for a while, you began to form relationships and they felt more like family than clients.

"Surprise!" I was totally shocked to see Cassandra, some of our clients and even Tamera all standing in the waiting area holding balloons, flowers and a cake that said WELCOME BACK HOPE.

"I can't believe you guys would do this for me" I said wiping tears from my face.

Cassandra came over and gave me a big hug. "I've been praying for you and Faith, I'm so grateful that you are back," she said.

I returned Cassandra's hug that was interrupted by Tamera pulling into a hug of her own.

"My best friend is back," Tamera said and I could hear the enthusiasm in her voice. "Now maybe I can have a life and find a husband too since I don't have to do everybody's hair in Charlotte anymore." We all laughed at Tamera, but I knew my best friend, she was serious.

I got my day started with one of my clients who refused to let anyone besides me cut her hair. After almost eight months of not having her ends trimmed caused her to get a short haircut. I found it very ironic that the thing she was trying to avoid thinking anybody else would have cut all of her hair off was just what she got from me. It felt good for someone to have that must trust in you, but if she would have let Cassandra or Tamera trim her ends, she wouldn't have had to go from shoulder length hair to an asymmetrical bob. Fortunately most of my clients allowed Sandra and Tamera do what needed to be done to their hair so when they sat back in my chair I didn't have any more challenges.

We were wrapping up our day finishing our last clients when my cellphone rang. I thought it was highly unprofessional to answer my phone and have a conversation while I was working on a client. I let the call go to voicemail as I finished curling my last client's hair. Two minutes later the phone rang again.

"You have a child now, you might want to get that," my client said.

The thought never crossed my mind that something could be going on with Faith. I put the curling iron back in the stove to heat up and picked up my phone. I saw that I had two missed calls and a text message from Shawn. I opened the text message hoping the reason he was calling was in the text message.

Call me ASAP

My heart rate sped up thinking something happened to my baby. I apologized to my client and went to the back room to call Shawn. He

answered on the first ring as if he was waiting on my phone call.

"Baby, what's wrong? Is Faith okay?" I asked panic evident in my voice.

I could hear him sigh through the phone. No bae, it's nothing like that. Faith is fine. I just got off the phone with my dad. It's my little brother."

"Oh my God, is he okay?" I asked relieved Faith was fine, but now concerned about Shawn's brother.

I just imagined Shawn sitting rubbing his hand over his face, I could hear the stress in his voice. "Eric is up there about to give my dad a heart attack. This boy has lost his mind."

I could only imagine what his sixteen year old brother had gotten into. Teenagers these days had a lot more issues than we did at that age. From the conversations Shawn and I had, I could tell his brother was resentful that he never knew their mother.

I was almost scared to ask for details, but I knew I needed to be supportive. "Baby, what exactly happened?" He got so quiet, I thought the call got disconnected. "Hello" I said making sure he was still there.

"I'm sorry baby, I'm just so mad right now. Eric got caught school at school with marijuana and got arrested," he said signing into the phone.

"What!" I yelled into the phone. "You can't be serious right now. What is your dad going to do?"

I hadn't met Mr. King yet, but I had talked to him on the phone several times. He seemed like such a good father, very supportive of his boys. He lost his wife and never remarried, just focused on raising his sons.

"I'm not sure what dad is going to do yet," Shawn said. "But for tonight, Eric sits in jail. I told Dad to leave him right where he was at. I just needed to hear the voice of my future wife to help calm me down."

As devastating as what I had just heard was, the last thing Shawn said put a smile on my face.

CHAPTER 24

Christmas was soon approaching and I had so many reasons to be excited. Not only was it Faith's first Christmas but it was also the day Shawn and I decided to get married. We finally found a house we both liked and had already started moving things in, but wouldn't spend our first day there until Christmas. I just prayed that with everything that was going on with Shawn's brother our plans didn't get altered. It took a lot of work to get a wedding planned in less than two months, but with myself, my mom, and my friends working together we got it accomplished.

I was really nervous to meet my future father and brother-in-law. It had only been Shawn, his father, and his brother for so long, I hoped they accepted me and Faith as a part of their family. The more Shawn told me about his brother, Eric, the more I prayed for him. He had started getting in trouble at school when he was about 10 for minor things, and it's been a downward spiral since then. I couldn't imagine growing up without mother. Eric was so young when their mother passed he had no recollection of her. It made me wonder if that was the root of his issues.

According to Shawn, their father had done everything in his power to give them a normal, happy life. He hadn't even dated another woman for fear of what his sons may think. When Eric began getting in trouble their dad had become so consumed with Eric's life, he forgot to have one of his own.

We still had a few weeks to prepare for the arrival of Shawn's family when I decided to have a dinner so they could meet and get to know everyone prior to the wedding. I was sitting at the dining room table having a cup of coffee trying to think of a place big enough to have this dinner when my phone rang. Happy to see Shawn's face on my screen, I picked up ready to hear the voice of my future husband.

"Hello," I sang into the phone.

"Hey beautiful," Shawn said causing me to blush. "I just talked to dad. They will be here as planned. Eric is home so they will be here in two weeks," Shawn told me and I was relieved we didn't have to rearrange anything. We didn't want the wedding to take place without Shawn's dad being there, and I was actually looking forward to the two weeks they would be spending with us so that Faith could start bonding with her grandfather and only uncle.

"So, what exactly happened with Eric?" I asked.

Shawn sighed into the phone before he told me what happened. "The amount of weed that he had on him wasn't enough to charge him with intent to distribute. He got probation and has to attend a drug program."

I thought that was fair, but I was sure Shawn didn't agree so I decided to ask. "How do you feel about that?"

He gave another sigh as he began to voice his opinion. "I think Eric is going to feel like he got away with something major and he's going to continue on this self-destructive path because there has been no real consequences. It's not fair to my dad. He's been taking this boy back and forth to counselors and therapist for the past six years, now he has to add taking him to see a probation officer to all the other appointments he has."

I really didn't know what to say and I didn't want to say the wrong thing and make Shawn upset, so I said the only thing that could possibly work at this point. "Baby, let's pray."

Shawn led us in prayer as we brought Eric before our heavenly Father. "God I'm asking now to please cover my baby brother with the blood of your son Jesus Christ. Order his steps that they may be pleasing in your sight. Deliver him from corrupt companions. Please fill my father with your peace. In the name of Jesus, amen."

I was so thankful the way God had worked things out for me and Shawn. That gave me the faith that I needed to believe that he would work a miracle into Eric's life as well. I ended my phone call with Shawn ready to put plans in motion for a big dinner so we all could meet my newest family members.

CHAPTER 25

I was so impressed with the way Shawn embraced his
relationship with God. He was true to his word about joining the
church. Even Pastor Wright was pleasantly surprised with his
spiritual growth. Shawn and I were on our way to our last
counseling session with Pastor Wright. I was in the passenger seat
of his Armada while he drove with one hand and held my hand
with the other. God how I loved this man. I felt like a child
counting down to Christmas hoping Santa Claus left everything
under the tree that was on their list.

"What's on your mind beautiful?" Shawn asked me
interrupting my thoughts.

I took a second to admire my soon to be husband as he
maneuvered through traffic. "I was just thinking about how much I
love you," I said laying my head back on the headrest.

He brought my hand up to his lips and gently kissed it. "I
love you more," he said as he parked in front of Victorious Life
Ministries.

We walked hand in hand into the side entrance of the
church so we would be closer to the pastor's office. Pastor Wright
met us just as we were walking in and greeted us both with a hug.

"You two go on in my office, I'll be in there shortly I just
want to see how choir rehearsal is going," she said as she made her
way to the sanctuary.

Shawn and I went into her office and sat in the two chairs
in front of her desk. Being in this office brought back so many
memories of when I was new to Christ and Pastor Wright took a
personal interest in me. We would spend hours in this very space
crying out to God for me. God really used her to save my life.

There was no way I could have continued drinking, clubbing, and being promiscuous without great consequence and I was so grateful God sent me to this woman of God.

"Okay, I'm back. I'm so sorry about that," Pastor Wright said as she came in and closed the door. "I just appointed a new praise and worship leader and some of the members of the praise team are giving her a hard time," she said as she walked toward us. Shawn and I stood up knowing that Pastor would start the session with prayer.

We held hands as she began to pray. "Merciful Father, first we give thanks, thanks for who you are, thanks for brand new grace and mercy, thanks for this union that you have put together. We thank you for giving us the gift of marriage. Thank you, God, for being an ever present help for Shawn and Hope. Help them to know that their help comes from you.

Cover their precious daughter with the blood of Jesus and use her oh God, even at a young age. Let their story be a testimony to many. We love you and honor you, in the name of Jesus, amen."

"Since today is our last session, do either of you have anything particular you want to talk about or pray about or just any unanswered questions for me?" Pastor Wright asked taking her seat in the chair behind her desk. Shawn and I looked at each other, neither of us prepared for such an unstructured session. Pastor must have sensed our apprehension. "You two have done so good on all of the assignments and homework, I figured I'd make the last session less intense," she told us.

Pastor Wright had us doing things like giving each other instructions while the other was blindfolded, writing each other letters, and going to the grocery store for each other with no help from the other, and that's just to name a few things we had to do. I did have to admit our communication had improved tremendously.

"I do have a prayer request," Shawn said reaching over to hold my hand. "My little brother is 16 and he's been getting in trouble for a while now, but recently it's gotten more serious. He got caught at school with marijuana, spent a little time in jail and is now on probation. My dad is getting frustrated with his behavior. So, I'd like to pray for my brother and my dad."

Pastor Wright sighed. "I'm so sick of the enemy trying to take our youth. Our young black men are definitely under attack. It's time for some spiritual warfare. The enemy is roaming the earth trying to devour our boys. One thing about this fight Shawn, is that it's not flesh and blood, it's not people that we are fighting, it's powers and principalities. It's not your brother, it's what is dwelling within him that we have to deal with. The enemy is using anything to get to these kids. This music, TV shows, movies, are just a few things the enemy is using to get to the kids. We have a few kids here at Victorious that have gotten in trouble and I had to accompany the parents to court. It just makes me sad."

Pastor Wright was silent for a few minutes before she spoke again.

"It's been my experience that the enemy doesn't go after people who have nothing to offer the kingdom."

Shawn gave Pastor a confused look. I knew just what she meant but I kept my mouth shut.

"What do you mean Pastor?" He asked leaning forward in his seat.

"Do you have a picture of your brother?" She asked and I could tell she was on the brink of a revelation.

Shawn pulled his phone out of his pocket and searched through his pictures. He put his phone on the desk and turned it to face Pastor Wright.

She picked up the phone and studied the digital image, she even enlarged the picture to get a better look. She continued to look at Eric's picture as she shook her head.

"Mmmmm Jesus, Jesus," was all she said over and over before she finally gave Shawn his phone.

"When will your family arrive in town Shawn?" Pastor asked.

"Next week, and they are spending Eric's whole Christmas break with us," Shawn answered looking between me and Pastor.

"I definitely need to meet your brother, I'd love to spend some time with him and see if I can get in his head," she said looking at both of us.

"The enemy wouldn't be trying him so hard for no reason. God wants to use your brother and the enemy has set traps up with his name on them trying to stop God's plan. But Jeremiah twenty-nine and eleven says God knows the plan for our lives and those plans are to prosper us, not harm us. Whatever I can do to help with him, please let me know. In the meantime, I will be praying for your brother's deliverance and your father's strength."

Pastor Wright led us in a powerful prayer that should have had the enemy scared to touch any young person, especially Eric. But the holy Spirit spoke to me and I wasn't sure how to receive what I heard. The second time the voice was louder and clearer, "put on your full armor daughter, this is war."

I knew right then that we just made the enemy mad.

CHAPTER 26

It was one week away from Christmas, the day that Shawn's dad and brother were coming to Charlotte from Springfield, Maryland. I was at the new house along with my mom, Faith, Chloe, and Tamera cooking and putting up Christmas decorations.

We found a house in Huntersville which was right off interstate four eighty-five on the outskirts of Charlotte. It was going to be quite a commute for Shawn, but he had already started looking for transfer opportunities at schools closer to our new home. There was no way we could pass up this house. It was two stories with three bedrooms and a bonus room that we could use as a bedroom if we chose to. There was a bathroom in the master bedroom with a double vanity, garden tub and separate shower. The selling point for me was the fenced in backyard, somewhere Faith could play when she got older.

I had just put Faith in her swing hoping it would help her fall asleep. With my mom, having her a majority of the time, she felt like everyone else had to hold her all the time like my mom did. I made a mental note to talk to my mom about that later. I was trying to put the finishing touches on the Christmas tree so I could help in the kitchen when my phone rang. I reached in my pocket and pulled out my phone to answer it. Always happy to hear my future husband's voice, I couldn't answer fast enough.

"Hi baby," I said with a huge smile on my face.

"Hey beautiful," he said into the phone sending shivers down my spine. "I was just calling to see if you ladies needed any help, I still have a few hours until my dad and Eric arrive" he said.

"If you want to come entertain your daughter that would be great, you know my mom got her spoiled rotten. I don't have to do much because she wants to be held twenty-four seven," I said glad that I would be able to get a lot more accomplished with Shawn being there.

"I will be there in about fifteen minutes. But there was another reason I called, I just wanted to thank you for agreeing to be my wife," he said and I could hear the emotion in his voice.

"You can thank me for the rest of your life, now hurry up and get here," I said before I hung up the phone.

With Shawn there taking care of Faith, we finished everything a lot sooner than expected. All of the food was done and ready to be served. There was ham, fried chicken, baked chicken, collard greens, green beans with potatoes, potato salad, rice and gravy, macaroni cheese, and rolls. For dessert my mom made a few of her famous sweet potato pies and a peach cobbler.

We had an eight foot Christmas tree that I decorated with red and gold ornaments in the living room. The lights from the tree made the whole room glow. Shawn even found time to put lights up outside.

Christmas was already my favorite time of year, but with Faith being here and my wedding coming up, it was even more special.

Since the house was so far from my apartment I brought my and Faith's clothes to the house so we could change before the dinner. Shawn was on his way out to pick up his dad and brother from the airport. As he was walking out of the front door of our new home, he walked up to me and hugged me.

"Are you ready to meet your new family members?" He asked pulling back from our hug.

I looked up into his hazel eyes before I said anything. "I'm ready, but are you ready to deal with your Eric?" I asked hoping Shawn wouldn't be too hard on Eric.

Shawn must have known what I was thinking. "Baby, I know we have been praying for him, but I still want to hurt him," Shawn said.

I thought back to our conversation with Pastor Wright. "Remember what Pastor said, we are not fighting flesh and blood, but powers and principalities. It's not Shawn we are in war with, it's the spirit that's trying to overtake Eric that we are in war with," I said hoping Shawn would receive what I was saying.

He rubbed his hand down his face then looked at me and smiled. "That is why I love you Mrs. King," he said as he kissed me on the cheek, then the forehead and walked out of the door.

Just as I made my way downstairs after getting myself and Faith dressed, the doorbell began to ring.

"I got it," my dad yelled out.

I didn't even realize my dad was there, he must have gotten there while I was upstairs getting dressed.

As I got down the last stair my dad reached out to grab Faith from my arms, Pastor Wright walked in as my dad opened the door with his free hand.

"Hey Hope," she said embracing me. "This house is absolutely beautiful" Pastor said looking around.

"Thank you, let me take you on a tour Pastor," I said grabbing her hand and leading her to see the remainder of our home.

Once we were in the bonus room, which held no furniture because we weren't sure what we wanted to do with it, Pastor Wright began to speak.

"I'm really proud of you and Shawn, you all have come a long way and I must say I might have misjudged him. I think of you as a daughter and I just don't want to see you hurt. I am really impressed with the way he has handled things and his growth in Christ." I was really surprised to hear my pastor say that. So many people never admit they may have been wrong and that made me respect her even more.

By the time I had finished showing Pastor Wright the house, other people had began arriving. Chloe and Tamera had made it back and they both looked stunning. Chloe was still wearing her hair flat ironed straight and she wore a black fitted dress that stopped right at her knees with gold accessories. Tamera, of course was sporting her signature twenty-twenty inch Brazilian weave. She had on gray wide leg pants with a gray sweater and silver hoop earrings.

"You two clean up quite nicely," I complimented my two best friends.

"Thank you honey," Tamera said as she looked me up and down.

I twirled around so I could show off my red wrap dress that flared at the bottom. Tamera had just cut my hair back into my pixie the day before so it was still looking like I just left the salon.

"You are absolutely glowing, you look fabulous," Chloe said smiling at me.

"Thank you, I'm so excited about tonight," I said as I made my way from the front door to the living room to greet my other guests.

Cassandra and Ms. Claire were sitting on my brand new black leather sectional sofa when I walked into the living room. I wasn't surprised to see that Faith had made her way into Cassandra's arms.

I walked over to get my baby girl from Cassandra when Ms. Claire spoke. "It's my time with Faith next young lady and I must say you look beautiful by the way. I love Faith's little red dress, she is so adorable."

I couldn't help but to smile at both compliments. "Thank you, Ms. Claire," I said. We had grown extremely close since my hospital days and I considered her a part of my family.

Since Faith was content with being the center of attention, I decided to check on my mom in the kitchen. She was busy placing the food in serving dishes.

"Mom, do you need some help?" I asked, secretly hoping she would say no because I didn't want to get anything on my dress.

"No pumpkin, your dad is placing these dishes in the dining room, besides we wouldn't want you to mess up that pretty dress," she said then winked at me.

I had to laugh at that because I had always been anal about my appearance. My mom washed her hands in the sink and then sat at the kitchen table.

"Come talk to me for a minute," she said as she motioned for me to sit at the table with her. I got a little nervous knowing how conversations with my mom didn't always go well.

"I know you love Shawn, and he is so good to you and my grandbaby. I am elated he is making an honest woman out of you, but I do have a few concerns," my mom said.

I didn't understand why my mom would bring this up at that moment. I decided to find out what her concerns were so I could ease her mind as much as I could.

"What kind of concerns do you have?" I asked my mom.

My dad walked in to get the remaining serving dishes and my mom waited until he was out of the kitchen before she spoke.

"Are you ready to deal with the issues Shawn's brother has?" I just looked at my mom while I tried to think of an answer that would not come off disrespectful. Before I could say anything, she continued with her opinion. "That may be a lot for a new marriage to take on. I'm sure Shawn is going to be more hands on with his brother with everything he has going on. Have you all talked about Shawn's level of involvement?"

I had to stop my mom before she went any further. "Mom, Shawn is about to be my husband. That means whatever he is going through, I'm going through as well. It's my job to support him and if that means standing in the gap for his brother until he is delivered, then that's what I'll be was doing," I told my mom as I stood up from the table. "Mom, please make Mr. King and Eric feel welcome, they have been through enough," I said as I walked out of the kitchen leaving my mom alone with her thoughts.

CHAPTER 27

"Honey I'm home," Shawn yelled walking in the front door. I was so glad he finally made it and I couldn't get from the living room to the front door fast enough. "You are absolutely, positively the most beautiful woman in the world," Shawn said as he embraced me.

"Thank you," I giggled like a schoolgirl with crush.

"I hope those shoes are going on our honeymoon," he whispered in my ear referring to the red pumps I was wearing. I pulled away from Shawn when I realized we had an audience.

"Dad, this is Hope, your future daughter-in-law" Shawn introduced me.

"Paul King, I'm so happy to finally meet you Hope. I've heard so much about you, you seem to be good for my boy," Shawn's dad said pulling me into a brief hug.

"It's so nice to meet you Mr. King" I said.

"Mr. King, we are family, call me Paul," he said with the same smile as Shawn.

I saw where Shawn got his good looks from. He was the spitting image of his dad, the only difference was their eyes. Where Shawn had hazel eyes, his dad had dark brown eyes.

"Eric, come meet your sister-in law," Paul said motioning for Eric to come over to where we stood.

"Hi Eric, I'm so glad to meet you," I said hoping I sounded enthusiastic.

Eric was just as handsome as his dad and brother. His eyes were light brown and held so much sadness. His complexion was a little lighter than Shawn's and he wore his hair in an afro that looked like he took a sponge to make it curly and wild like the all the teenage boys were wearing now.

"Hey," was all the response I got from him. I looked from Paul to Shawn to see the frustration on their faces.

"Let's go meet everyone else so we can eat," I said leading them into the living room.

Paul had immediately fell in love with Faith and it looked as if the feeling was mutual for her. She had laid on her Grandpa Paul's shoulder and went to sleep.

"Let me put her down so we can eat," Shawn said picking up a sleeping Faith.

Shawn went to put Faith in her crib upstairs while the rest of us went to the dining room. Once Shawn came into the dining room, Pastor Wright asked everyone to join hands so she could bless the food. Everybody filled their plates and we ate until we couldn't eat anymore.

We were all sitting around the table talking and laughing. We all tried to include Eric in our conversations but we mainly got one worded answers. I knew he was probably bored being around us and told him he could watch TV in the living room. That was probably the best thing he heard all night because he was up and out of the dining room before I could ask him if he would need any help.

Pastor Wright pulled me and Shawn into the kitchen so we could talk in private. "I just wanted to let you two know I've been praying in the spirit since Paul and Eric got here. The enemy has had a glimpse of his future and wants him bad. He is hurt and broken and the enemy found a way in through his brokenness. We need to keep him covered in prayer. Shawn, we are in this together and we are going to pray your brother out of this." Pastor Wright was full of confidence when she spoke.

I was so grateful for my pastor and her compassion for other people. I knew this wasn't going to be easy, but I also knew where two or three were gathered in the name of Jesus he would be in the midst.

We returned to the dining room and it didn't look like we were missed much. I noticed that Paul moved to sit beside Cassandra and she didn't seem to mind. I lightly elbowed Shawn and pointed to what I was looking at. I saw a slow smile overtake his face as he leaned down and whispered in my ear. "It's about time Dad looked at a woman, he needs a life."

I looked up into those hazel eyes and smiled. I was so happy that all the hard work my mom and friends put in for this dinner was paying off. I had no clue there could be a possible love connection in the air. Cassandra had been divorced for quite a few years and both of her children were grown and lived out of state. It would be nice to see her with someone.

Chloe, Tamera, and I were in the kitchen putting the rest of the food away and washing dishes when my mom and Ms. Claire walked in.

"You girls go on and sit down, we will take care of the kitchen," Ms. Claire said taking a bowl out of my hand.

"You don't have to tell us twice," Tamera said walking out of the kitchen.

Chloe and I followed her into the living room. We all stopped in the doorway and said a collective awwwww. I didn't know Eric well at all but the scene before me gave me hope. Eric was sitting on the sofa asleep with Faith sleeping on his chest. He had a protective hand resting on her back. Shawn walked up behind me and put his arms around my waist and chuckled.

"What are you laughing at?" I asked enjoying the feel of being in his arms.

"I don't why this boy thinks he's a thug. I can already see he is going to have his niece spoiled rotten," he said as we both continued to look at Eric and Faith sleeping.

"Let me get her back in her crib," I said reluctantly pulling free from Shawn's arms.

I must have startled Eric because as soon as I tried to take Faith he sat straight up with wide eyes and tightened his grip on her.

"I'm sorry, the baby was in her crib crying and I didn't want to interrupt you guys so I just went and got her," he said never loosening his grip on his niece.

"No need to apologize, we want you to be able to bond with Faith. You are the only uncle so you have a very special role to play in her life," I told Eric as I sat down on the sofa beside him.
He just looked at me for a moment with sad, light brown eyes. "Really?" he asked.

I was silently asking God for the right words to speak. He seemed to be receptive to me and I wanted to be able to build a relationship with him and help him get on the right track.

"Really," I said as I noticed Shawn, Tamera, and Chloe had left us alone. I was glad we were alone hoping he would open up to me since the audience was gone. I wanted to use this opportunity that God had provided to let Eric know that I would do anything in my power to help him. "Uncles are a big deal, and you are the biggest deal because you are the only uncle. You are going to be Faith's biggest supporter and cheerleader besides me and Shawn. You will be the one to sneak her candy before dinner, drive her to the mall, and threaten all of her boyfriends," I said happy that I got a little laugh from him.

"We need you around, Faith needs you around, look at how you were the only one to hear her cry. That must be some uncle and niece bond I know nothing about," I said hoping he got what I was saying, I didn't want to just come out and bring up his issues during our first conversation. But I did want him to know that I was aware of what he had been doing lately. "Whatever you need from me, even if it's just to talk, I'm here," I said as I got up and gently took Faith from his arms. As I was walking out of the living room, Eric stopped me.

"Hope," he said and I turned around.

"Thank you" was all he said. But those two words just increased my faith that God would move in his life.

I hated to leave my new home, but Shawn and I agreed that we wouldn't spend our first official night there until Christmas. Everyone had left except for Paul, Eric, Shawn, and myself. I was actually happy to have a little alone time with my future in laws. I was enjoying stories Paul was telling me about Shawn's childhood when Eric and Shawn came downstairs. Shawn was holding Faith's diaper bag and Eric was holding a wide awake Faith.

"Looks like I'm going to be up all night." I said getting up from my spot on the sofa.

"Bae, why don't you let Faith stay at my place tonight?" Shawn asked me. "I have dad and Eric to help with the princess, besides I know you and Mrs. Val are tired after everything you did today," he said sounding very persuasive.

"Well, I can't argue with that," I said standing on my tiptoes to give Shawn a hug.

We made plans to meet at church for ten o'clock service the next day and I was surprised to hear Paul say that Cassandra would be worshipping with us. Shawn and I exchanged looks but didn't say anything. From what I learned in the few hours I'd got to spend with Paul and the things Shawn shared with me, I could see he had put all of him into his boys and now it was time for him to have a life.

CHAPTER 28

I had been enjoying getting to know Paul and Eric. I tried to spend as much time with Eric as I could and he seemed to enjoy our time as much as I did. I didn't see the Eric that Shawn told me about. I saw a sad young man looking for acceptance. I honestly believed he was trying to fill the void of never knowing his mother. I knew I could never take the place of Eric's mother, but I did know how to pray for him. I could tell Shawn had mixed feelings about me and Eric spending so much time together. It was just a few days before Christmas and Shawn and I were at my apartment getting ready to move the last few things to the house.

"I appreciate all the time you are putting in with my brother," Shawn said taping up one of the boxes.

"Why do I feel a but coming?" I asked looking directly at my future husband.

He sighed and put the tape down then sat at the dining room table where I was wrapping glasses to be packed.

"You don't know Eric, I don't want you to get your hopes up for him to disappoint you. You don't see what dad and I see when it comes to him," he said causing something to rise in my spirit.

"You are absolutely right, Shawn, I don't see what y'all see in Eric, and that may be a good thing. I don't know all of the negatives about him. I'm not frustrated with him like you and your dad. I want to see him as God sees him. Maybe God is using me because I have a fresh set of eyes," I said trying to keep my voice from showing my true emotion.

"What do you mean by that?" Shawn asked clearly offended.

I stood up and started pacing the floor. "It's almost as if you and Paul have already counted Eric out, and that's what he feels. In Eric's mind, he has no reason to do better or try to change. Why change if you are only doing what people expect of you? He is a good kid with a good heart that just happens to be broken," I said with not caring how I sounded anymore.

In that moment, I knew what I had been praying for had been totally wrong. As soon as the words broken heart left my lips I felt a release in my spirit. I needed to be praying for a healed heart. His heart was broken early in life and no one seemed to understand that. Everyone was so focused on his behavior instead of trying to find out why he behaved they way he did. I had to talk to Pastor Wright, we had been prayer partners for Eric every day since the last pre-marital counseling session. I believed this breakthrough was the beginning of his deliverance.

Shawn got up from the dining room table and stood directly in front of me. He put his arms around my waist and kissed me on the forehead.

"I'm sorry baby," he said kissing me again on the forehead. "I love the way you are fighting for my brother. It's just that Dad and I are tired and it's been hard to fight for someone who doesn't seem interested in fighting for themselves," he said looking down at me.

I pulled back a little so that I could get a good look at Shawn when I said what I had to say. "I really believe that one of the reasons I am in your life is because of Eric. I just see what God wants to do in his life, I'm choosing to see him how God sees him. I choose to call him what God is calling him. It's actually a good thing that I don't know everything about his past so I have nothing to hold against him," I said trying to read Shawn's facial expression.

"You know what just hit me?" Shawn asked. He never gave me the chance to respond, he just kept talking. "What if everything that happened with the breakup, and Alana, and coming so close to losing Faith was all planned by the enemy to try to keep you from crossing paths with Eric?"

I thought about what Shawn just said and it was all starting to make sense. This was never about us as a couple. This was all about Eric's deliverance.

"Now you are getting what I'm saying bae," I said and gave him a hug and a sloppy kiss on the lips. "You know we have our work cut out for us right?" I asked sitting back down at the dining room table to finish packing my glasses.

"As long as I have my beautiful wife and daughter by my side I'm up for the fight," he said moving the already packed boxes by the front door.

"Eric really does admire you and he is so good with Faith. I've never seen him care about anything until I began seeing him with her," Shawn said as he took the last box of glasses and placed it with the rest by the door.

I had to laugh because I could already see where this was going. "You know that girl is going to have her uncle wrapped around her chubby little finger. But I think that's good for him, it's like he has a purpose now," I said.

Shawn came and sat at the table in the chair across from mine and grabbed my hand. "I do love the bond those two are forming, even though she barely wants to be bothered with me anymore," he said with a fake frown on his face. "I'm just hoping he doesn't go back to his old ways when they get back to

Maryland," he said squeezing my hand. This was the open door that I had been waiting on. I just hoped Shawn didn't think I was overstepping my boundaries.

"Baby, speaking of going back to Maryland, Eric has mentioned to me a few times he would like to stay in Charlotte. I didn't know how you and your dad would feel about that, but I promised him I would at least talk to you, but that's the most I could do for now. He was scared to come to either of you himself," I said looking down at our intertwined hands, avoiding eye contact.

"What makes him think that being here will be different?" Shawn questioned me.

I thought for a moment before I responded. "He says it's hard for him because of his friends. According to him all of his friends smoke, sell or both. Did you know one of his friends tried to get him to hold a gun for him? I told him I was proud that he stood up for himself because that could have ended up detrimental."

Shawn ran his hand down his face showing me he was frustrated and stressed. "I knew it was bad, but actually hearing how bad it really is, is not easy. I'll talk to my dad about it. I'm not sure he will want to move down here, but maybe we could take Eric for a while," he said and I could almost see the wheels turning in his head. "That's only if you are okay with him being with us," Shawn said.

I was elated that he was the one who suggested that and not me. I was more than grateful that he was open to the idea of Eric being in Charlotte. I had even started researching the high schools in the area, that's how much faith I had that things would work out in Eric's favor. We just sat there for a few minutes lost in our own thoughts. We started to speak at the exact same time.

"You go first," I said to Shawn.

"I was just sitting here thinking how much I love you and what an amazing woman you are for being so invested in my brother. I can see you really do care for him and that makes me love you more than I could have ever imagined possible."

The words he spoke caused my heart to swell and I was having a hard time keeping my emotions under control.

"I love you too and that's why I love Eric, he is a part of you. Your dad and Eric are my family now and I will do anything for them. I see so much in Eric and I know God has called me to fight in the spirit for him," I said wiping tears from my cheeks.

"We better get moving bae," I said getting up from the table.

We were moving the last of my things that needed to be taken to our new home. Chloe invited me to stay with her the next few days so that I could get everything out of my apartment and turn my keys in before Christmas. Faith had been staying with Shawn, Paul, and Eric a majority of the time so I didn't have to worry about her. Thank God for my support system, I don't know what I would have done without them, and I hoped I never had to find out.

CHAPTER 29

The day had finally arrived when I would become Mrs. Shawn King. It seemed like there were so many things to do before the wedding and I was getting more and more anxious by the minute. My mom, Tamera, and Chloe kept trying to reassure me that everything was running smoothly and they had everything under control. Since Tamera and Chloe were my maids of honor, Cassandra took on the task of doing all of our hair. My mom was still wearing her boy short natural so there wasn't much to do to her salt and pepper hair so she opted to keep an eye on Faith and get her ready.

I was getting nervous because the makeup artist that I hired for the day was running late. She came highly recommended and after seeing her portfolio I didn't mind paying double what she normally charged being that it was a holiday. It was at least a thirty-minute drive from the salon to the church and I didn't want to take any chances of being late to my own wedding. With us getting married on Christmas, we chose a time early enough so everyone involved could still enjoy any family traditions they had. I kept looking out of the window in the front of the salon looking for a car to pull up.

"Hope, calm down and have a seat, Nikita will be here," Cassandra said referring to the now twenty-minute late makeup artist. I was feeling very uneasy and I was hoping it was only due to Nikita being late.

I began looking in my bag to see what type of makeup I had just in case I had to do my own. Cassandra stopped working on Tamera's hair and walked to my station where I was digging through my bag. She began rubbing my back in an effort to comfort me.

"Tamera why don't you call Nikita and see if she's close. I don't need this girl over here trying to do her own makeup," she said still rubbing my back.

I sat down in my styling chair silently praying nothing else would go wrong.

"She said she is ten minutes away, there was an accident on eighty-five," Tamera informed us and I could have sworn I heard a collective sigh of relief throughout the room.

"Now Cassandra get back over here and finish my hair, and Hope stop digging in that bag and sit back and relax," Tamera demanded.

I should have been relieved that Nikita was on her way but I still had that uneasy feeling. I assumed it was just wedding day jitters so I tried my best to calm down. We heard the door of the salon open and I made my way to the front.

"I am so sorry I'm late," Nikita said walking in the salon with her rolling makeup case. "It was an accident on eighty-five, an eighteen wheeler overturned and it was down to one lane. I just pray that the driver is okay," she said as she wheeled her kit into the main area of the salon.

"You can set up at my station," I told Nikita pointing to my work area.

"Mom, you should go first so that you and Faith can go on to the church and make sure everything is set up," I said trying to take charge of the most important day of my life.

Nikita seemed to make up for lost time with her skill and speed. My mom's makeup was flawless and she was out the door with Faith in less than thirty minutes.

Once I saw myself in the mirror, I was so glad I didn't attempt to do my own makeup. I always thought of myself as an attractive woman, but the vision before me was breathtaking. I couldn't wait for Shawn to see me, I was tempted to send him a picture, but I didn't want to break any traditions.

"Nikita, you are absolutely amazing, I love what you did," I said praising her work.

"I had a great palette to work with," she humbly said. "But just wait until Cassandra hooks up your hair, you are only halfway done. I definitely need to add you to my portfolio, that is if you don't mind," she said as she began to clean up.

"Of course, I don't mind. Make sure you leave some cards so that we can refer our clients to you when they are in need of a makeup artist," I told her always ready to promote other women in the beauty industry.

As I sat in Cassandra's chair for her to curl my hair I finally began to relax. I decided to check my phone since I was so preoccupied with Nikita running behind, I hadn't looked at it in a while. I had a text from my mom saying everything was done and there was no need for me to worry. That eased my mind even more and the nervousness I was feeling before was replaced with excitement. Just as I was about to put my phone up my text message alert went off. I open the text to see that Shawn sent me a message.

You are the love of my life. You have made me a better man. I am ready to spend my eternity with you Mrs. King.

The only thing I could do at the moment was smile. I could not ask God for anything else, I had a beautiful healthy daughter and I was about to marry the man of my dreams. I responded to Shawn's text as Sandra put the finishing touches on my pixie.

Our eternity starts today Mr. King. I love you more than you will ever know.

"Okay Hope, I think we got you ready to walk down the aisle," Cassandra said as she handed me the hand mirror so I could see my hair from all angles.

I gasped when I saw how I looked with my makeup and hair done.

The gray smoky eyeshadow that Nikita chose gave my brown eyes a mysteriousness that I liked. My skin was glowing and the pale pink lipstick I had on accentuated my full lips. Sandra had my hair in a nineteen twenty's inspired finger wave style with curls framing my face like Betty Boop.

"Thank you so much Nikita and Cassandra. Words can't express how grateful I am to you two," I said as I got out of Casandra's chair.

"It was my pleasure Hope. I love being a makeup artist, but brides are my favorite, and a Christmas bride is even more special," Nikita said turning Tamera to the mirror.

"Girl you got me looking like a model, I thought I did my makeup pretty good up until now, way to lower a girl's self-esteem," Tamera said laughing at her own joke.

"I see you over there with your twenty-two inches, I'm going to need you to hook me up soon, I hear you are the lady to see for a sew-in," Nikita said motioning for Chloe to have a seat.

"We will definitely be staying in touch," Tamera said.

Once Chloe was done getting her makeup done and Cassandra pinned her loose curls up, we were able to leave for the church.

"I'll be there shortly girls, I need to take my rollers out and straighten up in here before I leave," Cassandra said pulling rollers out of her hair.

"Let me do your makeup really quick, I don't mind," Nikita said putting her makeup case back down.

"You know you want to be cute for Mr. Paul," Tamera said with a sly smile on her face.

I was thinking the same thing but didn't want to be the one to say something. Cassandra gave Tamera a look that was supposed to be serious but turned into a shy school girl grin. I was glad that Cassandra met someone she was interested in, since her divorce she put her all into making the salon successful, but it was time for her to have a life outside of the salon.

"Nikita, thank you, but you don't have to stay any longer. I know you want to get home to celebrate Christmas with your family," Cassandra said always considerate of others.

"Oh girl please. I don't have any family here so I was just going home to binge watch television," Nikita said and I could hear the sadness in her voice.

"Why don't you come to the wedding?" I asked. I couldn't imagine being all alone on any holiday especially Christmas.

"Oh no, I couldn't intrude on your day," she said applying foundation to Cassandra's already flawless skin.

"Please come, it would mean a lot to me," I said heading for the door.

"I'll text you the address of the church and hopefully we will see you there," I said.

I walked out of the salon with my two best friends in the world ready to marry the man my dreams were made of.

CHAPTER 30

Pastor Wright allowed me to use her office to get ready for this special occasion. That was one of the perks of being the spiritual daughter of your pastor. I felt so at peace while in her office because of the anointing that rested like a cloud of glory in that sacred space. This was a good sign for me since Shawn and I successfully completed our premarital counseling in this very space.

Tamera and Chloe came in dressed in their strapless knee length black dresses. Even though the dresses were the same, they looked completely different on them. Tamera's height and slender build made the dress a little shorter on her. All of Chloe's curves were on display and her dress stopped a little below the knee with her being shorter. But they were both stunning and I was proud to have them stand with me. I handed them both a gift bag.

"This is just a small token of my thanks for dealing with me through this whole process, I can't believe we ended up here and I'm so happy y'all stood by my side the whole time," I said trying to keep my tears under control.

"Oh, this is beautiful," Chloe said holding up the white gold necklace with a heart pendant that I picked out for her and Tamera.

"Thank you Hope," Tamera said fastening the necklace around her neck. Chloe followed suit with her necklace.

"Now let's get this dress on you," Chloe said getting my dress off the door of Pastor Wright's closet.

"Where is my mom?" I asked. "She would never forgive any of us if she missed me getting in my dress," I said.

"She said she would be in here in a few minutes, she was feeding Faith," Tamera informed me.

We passed the time by reminiscing on some of the things we had been through. Looking back on some of my past experiences I had to thank God from where he brought me from.

My mom finally made it to Pastor's office and not a moment too soon. I didn't realize how little time we had left before the ceremony.

"Mom, what took you so long?" I asked unzipping my dress bag.

"Your spoiled daughter, that girl already knows how to get her way," my mom chuckled.

"We have to make an honest woman out of you, so let's get moving," she said. Her sarcasm wasn't lost on me but I refused to let that one comment ruin the best day of my life.

As I began to pull my dress on, I began to feel nervous all over again. I assumed it was because it was only minutes away from the ceremony.

Once I was zipped up I looked in the full-length mirror and put my hand over my mouth in an attempt to control my emotions. The mermaid style dress with the sweetheart neckline made me look sophisticated and I hoped Shawn was as impressed as I was. Tamera pinned the small birdcage veil to my hair and ensured it was placed just right. My mom stepped in front of me and I admired the cream jacket and flared skirt she had on.

"You are beautiful daughter, and I really am proud of the woman you have become," she said with tears streaming down her face.

It was as if I had lived my whole life to hear my mom say she was proud of me.

"Thank you, mom," I said hugging her.

Tamera came rushing over with tissue for both of us. "Remember your makeup ladies," Tamera said handing us both a tissue.

We all took one last look in the mirror and we were heading out of the office so we could take our places when there was a frantic knock on the door.

"We know we are coming out now," Chloe said opening the door to find a startled looking Shawn with tears running down his face. That uneasy nervous feeling I had been fighting all day came back like a vengeance. I slowly walked toward Shawn afraid of what he was going to say.

"Baby," I said my voice trembling with fear.

He grabbed onto me for dear life and cried like a baby. I closed my eyes and rubbed his back.

"Just tell me baby," I said pulling back to look in his eyes.

I had never seen Shawn this way and nothing could have prepared me for the next words he spoke.

"We have to get to the hospital; my baby brother has been shot."

To Be Continued...

CPSIA information can be obtained
at www.ICGtesting.com
Printed in the USA
LVOW13s1830180518
577693LV00010B/444/P